STOLEN GOBLIN BRIDE

EMMA HAMM

For you, dear reader.
Always for you.

CHAPTER 1

*E*sther knew when the birds stopped singing that something dangerous had entered the forest.

Her father had taught her when to hide before he disappeared along with her mother. She still didn't know why or where they had gone. Their story was muddled in her head, but she liked to think they'd gone on some wild adventure rather than losing their lives to a beast in the wood.

They had taught her the forest was dangerous. The trees could talk to each other if they wanted to, and when they did, she should listen. Magical greenery grew through the mud, and the loam was kind-hearted and good.

But the birds? She had to be wary of the birds.

Blowing her tangled nest of blonde curls out of her vision, she straightened and eyed the shadows in the forest. The tall pillars of trees were stately guards, standing ready to warn her of any attack. Slashes of sunlight illuminated even the darkest of shadows. She was here at the right time. No beasts emerged from the darkness at high noon. So why had the birds stopped singing?

She could hear a faint sound on the breeze. The slightest of chimes, that was... well. Beautiful. The music called to her like a siren on the rocks of the sea, and Esther stepped closer to the song.

Her mushroom filled basket fell from her hands. She hardly noticed the plunking of all her hard work falling to the ground. The moss squished beneath her toes, shoes forgotten in the roots of a nearby tree, but she didn't mind. Esther preferred to be barefoot, anyway.

The sound drew her all the way through the woods to a small clearing where daisies grew on the ground in bunches. Like a magical being had laid out tiny bouquets while waiting for her.

It was within this sun soaked meadow that she saw the goblins. They came to market every year with their strange wares and odd looks. Though they mostly wore cloaks, Esther had peeked beneath a few of them before. The goblins were terrifying mashed creatures of man and beast. But she liked them all the same. Even though her sister, Freya, said she shouldn't.

Esther always had an easier time with animals than with people. They made more sense and were easier to understand.

So when she saw the rickety carts weren't yet decorated to beckon the unwary buyer, it was like a gift. The goblins weren't trying to lure her to their camp. They were merely seated around a small ring of stones with a fire crackling within. One of them held a flute in his hands and carefully blew into it with cat lips and whiskers that danced with each breath.

She couldn't even see what they were selling. And they likely wouldn't want her to see just yet. They were, after all, particularly good salesmen if a person didn't know how dangerous it was to buy their goods.

Goblin deals never ended well for humans. Her sister claimed that Esther might buy jewelry from them, but then would pay with her firstborn child. And Esther would never know that was the price until it was too late.

Who would want a firstborn child, anyway? A baby seemed like a lot of work.

One goblin had his head underneath the cloth of the cart, one foot lifted as he wiggled to get something. That was when Esther saw his tail. A long rat tail weaved as he struggled, and she couldn't stop the gasp from escaping her lips. The sight of him was so strange, so unusual, that she entirely forgot she should hide from the goblins. Just in case.

All the sounds in the meadow stopped. The birds had already made it clear they would not sing while these odd creatures took over their glen. Now, the cat goblin stopped playing his flute and all the other goblins froze.

They stared as one at the young woman who stood silhouetted by the forest beyond.

Esther must have looked a sight. The hem of her pale green skirts was dipped in mud and filth. She had twigs in her wild blonde hair. Her cheeks were likely ruddy from hard work in the wilderness all day, so she certainly appeared like some wild thing from the forest had happened upon them. Perhaps that would benefit her.

3

Maybe these terrifying creatures would cast pity on the poor, mad girl who stumbled upon their camp.

"Ah ha!" The rat tailed goblin shouted as he pulled himself from underneath the cart's cover. "I knew I put it in here, Horace! Obviously, I wouldn't have left home without it..."

His words trailed off at the end as he caught sight of Esther standing not twenty paces away. He was... well. More strange than she'd expected. The tail still waved behind him, but his face was even odder. Though he had the features of a mortal man, his nose was too elongated to appear normal. He looked like someone had mixed a man and a rat together and voila. Here he was.

The rat goblin's mouth slowly dropped open as he continued to stare at her, and the item in his hand thudded to the ground. Esther's attention flicked to the glittering piece of jewelry. It was a rather impressive crown dripping with gemstones the color of the sky.

"Oh," she said, her voice little more than a squeak. "You shouldn't let that touch the mud. You'll have to spend hours cleaning it."

He swallowed hard, then looked down at the crown. "My goodness. I dropped it."

A hulking goblin stood, one that looked much older than the others. He was more bear than man. He lumbered over to the rat goblin and picked up the crown with a low growl. "Lux, you idiot. You know this crown would bring us good coin! Now we'll never get the dirt out of it."

The rat-faced goblin—Lux, she reminded herself—looked so upset that she couldn't help herself. Esther cleared her throat and pointed to their right. "There's a stream over there. If the mud doesn't dry, you might have a chance."

Horace, for the large goblin could only be Horace, eyed her with a frown. "You're awfully nice for a mortal, but we'll take the help." He slapped the crown into Lux's chest and sent the young man back a few paces. "Go clean it. And you, girl, get out of here."

She should. Esther knew she should pick up one foot and turn herself around. Right back into the forest where she would hopefully find the basket she'd dropped like a fool. Freya would be so mad at her, and she was supposed to behave for a few days and not bother her sister.

But the boy's shoulders curved in and he nodded so sadly that she feared what would happen if he wandered off alone. He was just... he was so adorable like that. His ears were too big. His eyes were a little watery. All he'd wanted was to find the crown he said he'd brought, and this giant man was making him feel guilty for dropping it. All because she had startled him.

This was her fault. Esther needed to fix it.

Instead of wandering back into the forest, she turned and trailed the goblin boy. Sure, her footsteps might have been louder than she wanted, but he never looked over his shoulder. Not even once.

And when he made it to the stream, he crouched down and sullenly swished the beautiful crown in the water. Like he had no idea she was right behind him at all.

Esther stepped out from behind a tree and cleared her throat. Hopefully that wouldn't startle him too much.

Of course, this goblin boy was a little more jumpy than she'd expected. He flinched, dropped the crown into the water, and then pressed both his hands to his face in horror. "Oh no," he whispered. "Oh no, oh no, oh no."

Yet again, she ruined another of his tasks. Esther burst out of the trees and floundered into the water with all the grace of a bull. "I'm so sorry! I didn't think you'd drop it."

"Well, when a terrifying monster walks out of the woods, it's entirely normal to be frightened!"

She paused, one hand still fishing in the river while she craned her neck to stare up at him. "You think I'm a monster?"

Sure, she hadn't brushed her hair for the better part of a week. But Esther kept herself clean, even though her clothing was currently smeared with mud. She was still a pretty young woman, and the fact that he thought she was a monster was rather rude.

He straightened, eyes wide and nose twitching. "No, not a monster. That's the wrong word. Mortals are terrifying, you see. All your kind does is pick up weapons the moment they see a goblin, and I just don't want you to hurt me."

"Hurt you?" Her fingers wrapped around a metal frame and she tugged the now clean crown out from between two algae covered stones. "Do I look like I could hurt anyone?"

He eyed her again, but this time she could almost feel the heat of his gaze sweeping up her form. Esther wasn't sure anyone had ever stared at her like that. As if he were devouring every part of her body he could see. Finally, the goblin boy tilted his head and shrugged. "I have no idea what's underneath all those layers of clothing. You could have many weapons for all I know."

Underneath her clothing? No man had ever been so forward with her. Ever.

But she liked it. Esther's cheeks burned with embarrassment. She tucked a strand of hair behind her ear and tried to flirt back, although she'd never been very good at that. "I wouldn't hurt you even if I could. You seem like a good goblin."

Good goblin? That was all she could come up with?

Esther wanted to hit herself over the top of the head for even thinking to use those words. Now it sounded as if she viewed him like a dog, or a faithful pet.

She stumbled out of the water, slipping a few times on the slick rocks, before holding out the crown for him to take. "Here you go. Again, I'm sorry I caused so much trouble. I heard the sound of the flute and I couldn't stop myself from seeing where it came from."

This time the goblin boy smiled. He took the crown and wiped it off on his shirt, looking up at her through the dark locks of his hair. "I've heard ladies liked flutes. Never thought to learn how to play one until this moment."

Freya would kill her if she found out that Esther had spent this much time with a goblin. Her sister was very particular about what was right and wrong when it came to the goblin men that wanted to sell them items from their markets. But Esther wasn't planning on buying anything.

Besides, what would she do with a crown?

"I should get going," she whispered. She shook her skirts out even though they were waterlogged and heavy. "I hope you aren't in too much trouble over the crown. That would be a sad day. It's just a little dirt."

"A little dirt," he repeated with a soft smile. "I suppose you're right. Horace is very picky about the things we sell, though. He wants them to be perfect."

"From the few things I've seen, they usually are." The goblin jewelry was known throughout the world, and anyone who wore it had obviously paid a high price. Only nobles would dare wear something like that, though.

"My work is not anywhere near this." He gestured with the crown. "But I'd be honored if you wore one of my pieces around that lovely neck."

No. She couldn't. This was the trickery her sister had talked about. If she took anything from this goblin, then she would be forced into a life of servitude in the faerie realms. She'd become a goblin slave.

Esther licked her lips and quietly replied, "I don't think I can."

The goblin boy reached into his front pocket and pulled out a tiny necklace. The crescent moon swung on a silver chain, so similar to the one her mother had worn.

Esther gasped. She even could believe for a few moments that the necklace was the exact one she'd grown up loving. The very moon she'd stared at and played with as a child.

That was silly, and thinking those thoughts would only make her disappointed. So she shook her head and retreated. "I can't."

"Wait!" the rat boy called after her. "Will I see you again?"

"Never!" she shouted in reply. But as she crashed through the underbrush, Esther recognized the words ached like a gut clenching lie.

CHAPTER 2

*E*sther snuck back home without the basket of mushrooms. She already knew Freya would yell at her for losing something so important, even though they already had plenty of food for a little while.

But Freya was always worried about everything. Her sister feared the shadows in the night because their parents had made her so afraid of what could happen if she let down her guard for even a second. In contrast? They'd allowed Esther to run free through the forests and decide what she wanted to do.

What she wanted was to be a wild being that the villagers feared. Oh, she wasn't interested in magic or witchcraft. Her parents never would have let her stray that far from the path. But they had allowed her to enjoy the little things.

She watched dust motes and called them by faerie names. She built tiny homes in the bases of trees, hoping brownies would leave blessings for their family. And, mostly, her mother had ignored her oddities.

Freya, on the other hand, would have had such strangeness beaten out of her at a young age.

Esther opened the door to their small wooden home and winced as the hinges squeaked. She really needed to oil those if she planned to sneak inside without Freya noticing.

"Esther?" Freya called out. "Did you get the mushrooms I asked for?"

"Um." What was the story she'd come up with again? "Do you remember the boar Dad saw years ago? I saw it again today. And I had to drop the mushrooms while I ran away from it?"

A loud clanking sound echoed from the back of the hut. Who could guess what Freya was doing back there, but she came charging into the living room like goblins were nipping at her heels.

Her sister was the moonlight to Esther's sunlight. Dark hair, pale skin, not a freckle in sight. Freya looked like some storybook princess, while Esther looked like a mud child someone might have found in the forest. Of course, Freya's personality would dash anyone's hopes of her being a real princess. She was downright terrifying when she wanted to be.

"Did you say a boar?" Freya repeated, her eyes maybe a little too wild.

Apparently that story choice was too aggressive. Esther cleared her throat and shifted her weight from foot to foot. "Well, maybe it was a baby boar. I couldn't tell. I dropped the basket and ran before I could get a good look at it."

Now that she'd gone back on the story, she could see

11

that Freya's belief had disappeared. Freya narrowed her eyes and made a low humming sound in the back of her throat. "Right. Well, I suppose that's fine. We're going to market today, anyway."

"Why?" Esther didn't think they needed anything at the market. Or at least, Freya hadn't told her they did.

"We ran out of flour." And that was that. There was no arguing with her sister when she wanted something done. Esther had to tag along or she'd hear it for the better part of the next week.

Her legs were tired from tromping through the forest all day, but she followed Freya out of their small hut. A path led down toward a much larger ravine where the rest of the townsfolk lived. Her mother had claimed she preferred living away from others for their own safety. The townspeople knew nothing about the fae or their secrets. As such, their mother could only assume that the villagers wouldn't know how to protect themselves.

Their mother had even offered to create wards for some homes. She'd done everything she could to spread her knowledge, even when it was unwanted. An unprotected village near their home needed her help.

Freya didn't share the same concern. Her sister would rather leave everyone up to their own mistakes.

Trudging through the fields, Esther swallowed hard as she heard the goblin bells, yet again.

What were they doing here? So close to town?

They knew better than to tempt fate. Anyone could happen upon them, and an angry mob of mortals was dangerous even to the faeries themselves. They needed to sell their wares in more secretive places!

Clearly they didn't agree with her thoughts. The goblins were all where she'd hoped not to find them. They'd set up their jewelry and fruit on their rickety carts that were covered with layers of fabric and fur.

"Don't look at them," Freya hissed.

Her sister tossed her shawl over both of their heads, forcing Esther to no longer stare at the goblin men and women. But she could see through a small hole and noticed the rat-faced boy was among them. He stared as if two goddesses walked by him.

And Esther couldn't get the sight of him out of her head.

By the time they finished in the market, Esther had already made up her mind. She was going back to the goblin carts, and she was going to buy that necklace from him. Sure, it might not be her mother's necklace, but it was hers all the same. She needed something to remember her mother by.

With Freya already struggling with an armful of far too much produce, Esther stopped in the middle of the road and let out a loud, very dramatic shriek. An embarrassing amount of townspeople stopped to stare at her, including her sister, who wore a glare on her face that should have seared the flesh from Esther's bones.

"What are you doing?" Freya hissed. "That's quite enough of that."

"I lost my necklace." This was her plan. She would pretend to have lost a necklace in the village, and then when she returned home with a new one, Freya would be none the wiser.

"So?" Freya hefted the bag in her arms higher. "You

have so many of them, Esther. Put another one on when we get home. We don't have a lot of time before the sun sets."

"But this one is important to me! I can't just leave it." Esther tapped her toes on the ground, then turned around like she was going to take off either way. "I'll meet you back at home, Freya! It won't take me very long."

At least her sister didn't think Esther was in any danger in the middle of town. They knew everyone here, and even though some villagers thought the two sisters to be rather strange individuals, they wouldn't hurt her. No one here was bloodthirsty enough for that.

Esther ducked behind a building and slowly followed her sister out of the village. She waited until Freya disappeared over the rise that would take them to their small hut by the forest, and then she was safe. Freya couldn't turn around and see her, which meant Esther could actually talk to the goblins with no one scolding her. Or preventing her from buying the one thing she wanted most.

She approached the carts with determination and squared shoulders. Without hesitation, she marched right up to the bear-like goblin Horace and cleared her throat. "I want to buy the jewelry that was offered to me when I last saw you."

All the goblins stopped talking again. One of them even pulled back his hood, revealing a long beak with multi-colored feathers that stuck out of his face.

Horace glared down at her. He took his time eyeing her from head to toe and then snorted. "We give nothing away for free, Miss. Off with you."

"I have money." It wasn't much, but she had some left over from what her parents had left her. Sure, that money should have gone toward a dowry, if Freya had anything to do with it. But Esther never wanted to get married.

She wanted that necklace, though. And she'd snuck the coin out before they had left for the market.

Again, Horace narrowed his eyes on her and then snorted. "Then we don't want to sell to the likes of you. Hasn't anyone ever warned you about a goblin market, little one? It's almost too easy to steal a curse out of you."

"I don't want a curse. I don't want any magic either." Esther craned her neck and stood on her tiptoes, looking through the carts for the one necklace that she wanted. "The goblin boy from earlier. The one who had a rat tail. He offered me a necklace that I want very much."

If it was possible, Horace's glare burned with even more anger. "Lux!" he snarled. The shout clapped through the air like the crack of a whip, and the goblin boy came racing from behind one of the carts.

Breathing heavily, he looked between them with a wide-eyed stare. "What is it?"

"This girl said you offered her a necklace. What have I told you about goblin curses?" Horace grabbed him by one of his overly large ears and pinched.

Lux yelped and wiggled in the big goblin's grasp. "I wasn't trying to curse her! I didn't want her to buy the necklace. Giving isn't the same as buying. Now let me go!"

What was that supposed to mean? Freya had always told her a goblin deal was simple. If someone didn't pay what the jewelry or goods was worth, then they owed the goblins a debt. Plain and simple.

15

The necklace he'd shown her wasn't worth more than the gold coin she had in her pocket. What were they all so worried about? It wasn't worthy of a goblin curse, and she wouldn't owe a debt.

"I want the necklace," she said again. Esther made sure her tone was firm and there was no way any of them could second guess her intentions. "I want it and I will have it because it was already offered to me."

Horace released the goblin boy, Lux.

The young man's tail wrapped around his waist and he cleared his throat. "I'd rather give it to you, miss. If that pleases you."

No, it didn't. She didn't want to owe any goblin a debt. But considering the way these goblins were all glaring at her, she had a feeling paying wasn't on the table. She'd have to be sneakier than just giving him the coin if she wanted to avoid a goblin debt.

Squaring her shoulders, she took a deep breath and nodded. "That will satisfy me."

His eyes flashed, bright and hot. Lux reached into his pocket and pulled out the necklace. The beautiful piece dangled from his clawed finger. "Then it is yours."

She snatched it from his hand. "Esther. My name is Esther and thank you for this. It looks just like a necklace my mother used to wear."

A strange expression crossed his face, but he ducked behind the carts before she could attempt to hug him and sneak the coin into his pocket. That left only one route for her then. Esther sneezed loudly and left the coin on the cart he hid behind. Right on the very edge.

"Thank you everyone," she called out as she backed away. "I appreciate the jewelry. You have lovely work."

Horace growled at her and turned away. Such was the easiest transaction she'd ever had, and now she held a necklace just like her mother's in her hand. Esther even looked down at it to make sure it was the right one, and it was.

Goodness, it was beautiful. The silver was so delicately hammered that she knew it had been made with love and care. Sure, some of the more sparkly jewelry pieces were impressive, but Lux had created a simplistic jewelry piece that rivaled all those with glittering gemstones. The boy had talent. She could only hope the bear of a goblin saw that.

Esther whistled as she turned back to her home and clasped the necklace around her neck. Her day had turned out even better than she'd hoped, and that was saying something. She'd met goblins! For the first time. And they hadn't been as bad as her sister said.

"Wait!" The shout came from the goblin market. "Mortal girl! Wait!"

She turned around to see Lux sprinting after her. He held her coin in his hand, breathing hard with wild eyes. Even his tail lashed dramatically behind him.

"What is it?" she frowned, fear shuddering through her body. "Is that not enough?"

"No, no it would be fine, it's just..." He looked at a loss for words. "Why would you pay me? You said you knew what goblin curses were!"

She did. Freya had made sure that Esther knew every-thing about goblin curses and how to avoid them. Their mother had studied the Goblin kind for a very long time, and she couldn't have been wrong. Could she?

Stammering, Esther replied, "I... I... A goblin curse can only be from something stolen or given."

"No," he replied with a sharp snarl. "You foolish mortals. A goblin curse comes with anything a person buys from a goblin. It's dangerous to have our wares, but buying from us can end in tragedy."

Oh.

Oh no.

Esther gulped. "What can I do? I didn't know! I really didn't know, and I don't want to be cursed. I just wanted a necklace that looked like my mother's!"

Lux met her gaze with a haunted expression. His tail whipped at the air behind him, as though he already knew a fight was coming and he was battling on her behalf. Finally, he sighed and looked behind them. "There is no other way. I have to put a goblin curse on you, but the best I can do is give you time."

"Time for what?"

His next uttered word sent a chill through her very bones. "To run, Esther of Woolwich. I can only give you time to run."

So she did.

CHAPTER 3

*E*sther ran like the goblins were on her heels. She slapped through the branches and darted into their home, pressing her back against the door.

"Freya?" she called out. "I may have made a mistake!"

No one responded. Frantically she searched through the entire house for her sister, who always knew how to make things right, but all she found was a small note.

Went out to check the traps, hoping for a rabbit.

Be back in a few hours.

"Damn it," Esther muttered.

She'd have to figure this out on her own. What had the goblin boy meant? Run? Where was she supposed to go? Esther's heart raced in her chest at the mere implication that she needed to leave this hut.

This was where she had grown up. Her mother had rocked her to sleep in the chair by the corner. Her father had looked for monsters under the bed in the back room. And Freya, dear Freya, had given up all her own dreams just to make sure that her little sister was safe and happy.

And what had said little sister done? She'd squandered all these sacrifices and instead, she'd made a deal with a goblin that couldn't be undone.

Run. She had to run.

But where? There was nowhere in the world safer for her than right here. Surrounded by all the wards her mother had built after years of studying magic. This home was locked up tight from those of magical origins, and she could stay here forever.

That was fine. Esther could give up her sense of adventure as long as she didn't have to face those goblins. So that's exactly what she did.

When Freya returned, her sister was none the wiser that anything had happened at all. Esther smiled, she laughed, she even helped cook dinner which might have been a little suspicious. And when they went to sleep, she thought that was the end of it.

Until it wasn't anymore.

The goblins came for her the next afternoon, this time with a leader who wore a hooded cloak and rode on a pristine white horse. If they thought that would intimidate her, then they were sorely wrong.

Esther stalked to the very edge of the barrier and held the necklace out for the goblin boy to take. "I don't want it if you're going to follow me around. And you can't steal me away while I'm in here."

Poor Lux, he didn't look happy at all. His ears were already drooping and his hands were clutched over his heart. "I don't want to do this, but I do not know how to change what has happened. There are rules, Esther. Rules that even I cannot break."

She wildly gestured with the necklace again. "Then take it back! I'm giving it to you, that has to count for something!"

The man on the horse turned toward her and for a second, she caught a glimpse of a handsome face flashing with silver. "That's not how it works, little one. You are goblin property now."

"No!" The shout came from her sister, for it could be no one else. "Esther! Get away from them!"

Freya ran to her side in nothing but a towel, anger turning her usually pretty face into something to be feared. But Freya didn't even look at Esther. She was dragged into Freya's arms while her terrifying sister glared at the goblin on the horse.

After that, Esther didn't listen to anything her sister said. She stared at the rat-faced boy who looked at her with almost hope in his eyes. Like he wanted her to see past his face and to the young man underneath.

Though they might be different, he didn't want to hurt her. And he certainly didn't want her to be so afraid of him.

Somehow, that eased the sting of knowing he and his people hunted her. That she'd never be able to leave these lands, no matter what Freya did. The goblins wanted her.

And the goblins would have her.

Freya shook her hard. "Did you make a deal with them?"

"No." Esther snapped out of her strange trance, staring at the goblin boy. "No, I didn't. The necklace was a gift, Freya. A gift."

The argument that followed only made her head spin even more. Freya spoke to the goblin on the horse like they had seen each other before. And maybe that was a story she'd eventually hear.

But she was dragged back into their home before she knew it. Freya tossed her into the bedroom and refused to let her go. Her sister planned on staying up all night with a gun in her hand, ready to kill any goblin that stepped through their door. Esther didn't know how that would help. They were magical creatures, and surely a bullet wouldn't intimidate them. They could probably spell it so not a single bullet even struck them.

Besides, their mother's wards would hold. They always did.

As she lay on her bed, looking at the stars through their window, Esther pondered whether or not she even wanted to be here.

This hut on the edge of the forest was nothing more than a tease. Magic was too tempting. Esther had always wanted to see what it could do, or what she could do while using it. Magic was... Powerful.

Esther wasn't powerful.

She had been told her entire life to fear a goblin deal. They were monsters under the bed and hiding in the shadows of her closet, ready to snatch her away with their claws.

But she'd met them now. They were people with thoughts and ideas. Big bear men who growled at children. Boys with a talent for jewelry.

No manner of frustration or fear could change her mind. Though the goblins might be hunting her now, they were an opportunity for her to take control of her own life. What would happen if she went with them?

Danger, maybe.

Or perhaps adventures no human had ever experienced before.

She should have ignored the scratching sound on her window when the moon was at its highest peak. She didn't. Esther rolled out of bed and tiptoed to the glass pane, looking over her shoulder to see Freya still sat straight as a board, staring at the door.

Biting her lip, Esther eased the window open and thanked the heavens at least this part of the house wasn't so loud.

Lux stood on the other side of the window, wringing his hands and looking very much like a boy who had snuck out to see the girl he loved. Fanciful thought, really, but Esther found she quite liked the image.

When he noticed she'd opened the window, he cleared his throat. "Esther, I've come to steal you away."

She leaned an elbow on the window and propped her chin in her palm. "Where are we going?"

The shocked expression on his face was coupled with the most hilarious of blinks. He looked at her like she'd lost her mind. "What do you mean? I thought you'd be screaming and calling out for your sister to help."

"She's busy watching the door." Esther shrugged. "Besides, Freya knows how to take care of herself. I hardly think she'd notice if I left for a while."

"It won't be just a while." Lux frowned up at her, his brows furrowed. "A goblin deal is forever."

She looked one last time over her shoulder at her

sister and licked her lips. It was partly her job to keep Freya happy. And she knew that her sister would fall to pieces without Esther here. But this was an adventure of a lifetime right in front of her.

How many times had Esther stood in a field, turning in slow circles and wishing the faeries would come take her away? Her mother, father, and sister had all feared the realm they couldn't explain. But Esther had loved the fairytale with every beat of her heart. She'd always wanted to be more than just human.

Since she was a little girl, Esther had wished every night to be a faerie princess. An ethereal being full of magic and possibility. And this was her chance to become one of them.

She looked back out the window and nodded. "I know. Forever. So where are we going?"

His tail twitched behind him. "The faerie realm is not for the likes of you. I'm here to kidnap you while the other goblins deal with your sister. You do understand that, don't you?"

"I do." Esther searched for a bag to put her clothing in. She'd only need a couple dresses. The faerie realm was bound to have clothing she could wear, after all.

Scrabbling sounds proceeded his clawed hands on the windowsill as he dragged himself and peered over the lip. "Are you mad?"

"Quite possibly."

His overly large ears twitched, then laid back against his skull. "Are you dangerous?"

Esther flashed him a bright smile. "Certainly."

The goblin shuddered, and Freya was so happy she

could make him feel that uncomfortable. Any goblin might have taken her. Horace would have been terrifying, and that goblin on the horse... She didn't know what his story was, but he terrified her.

Instead, she'd gotten a goblin who was quite endearing in his odd ways. He acted like any boy she might meet in the village. Opposed to change and oddities, but strangely drawn to the wild young woman who lived in the woods.

She finished packing and threw the bag over her shoulder. Sliding toward the entrance to their bedroom, she peered at Freya in the hopes her sister was still none the wiser.

A goblin man stood in the center of her kitchen, his hands outstretched and shadows wrapping around Freya's head. The woodstove still burned. Freya still gripped the gun, but she stared like nothing was happening. As if she couldn't see the goblin man in front of her.

This powerful creature looked up and met Esther's shocked gaze. His skin was burnished like silver. His ears pointed. And when he smiled, he had sharpened teeth that flashed in the light.

No. She didn't want to be around that goblin. But she couldn't let him finish whatever it was he had started.

"Don't hurt my sister," she said. "I will not have her harmed for my mistake. The goblin boy is here, and I'm willingly being stolen."

"I don't plan on harming your sister at all, little girl. I want her alive because I think she will be an adversary to be admired." That grin never budged as he spoke. "Besides. You have a new life now as a goblin bride. Run along to your newfound keeper. You're his problem now, Esther."

Whatever that meant. She decided she didn't like this goblin, but also, that she didn't want to test him.

Gulping, she backed away from the kitchen and returned to her bedroom window. Lux stood outside still, his arms wrapped around his waist and his tail nervously tapping his leg.

"Are you ready?" she asked.

"For what?" He turned around, then his eyes widened as he watched her throw a leg over the windowsill. "What are you doing? Shouldn't you come out the front door?"

"It's not that high up." It was only as high as she was tall. All she had to do was grab onto the window sill and lower herself to the ground. Theoretically, it should be easy.

She situated herself, then swung the other leg over the ledge.

"Have you done this before?" Lux asked nervously.

Esther turned to look into the house and blew out a long breath. Last chance. She could stay here with her sister and everything would stay the same. But some voice in her head screamed that she needed to do this. Not for Freya. Not for their parents. Esther had to make a choice that was right for her, and if she didn't leave here now, then she never would.

She hadn't been born to sit in this little hut for the rest of her life with her sister. She'd been born to experience adventure. To feel what it was like to wander the earth and discover new things, people, and places.

"No," she replied, planting her palms on the

windowsill. "But no one ever knows if they're good at something until they try it."

Unfortunately, Esther had forgotten that she wasn't very strong to begin with. All of her strength was in her legs from walking every day. Freya was the one that worked in the gardens. Esther was too flighty and forgot too much. So, as she dropped all her weight onto her arms, her hands struggled to grip the wood.

She tumbled toward the ground, biting her lip hard to keep from screaming, only to be caught in mid air.

A long wheeze echoed between her lips in the mockery of a quiet scream as she stared into the eyes of the goblin boy who had caught her. A single lock of hair fell over his eyes and she hadn't realized how vivid they were. Sure, they might be brown. But those eyes had the ripples of mountains in them. She could see forever in his gaze. Adventures that went on for a lifetime.

"Thank you," she whispered.

"I told you not to climb out the window. You could have walked by the Goblin King." He held her so carefully with his arm behind her back and the other behind her knees. "This was an unnecessary risk."

"But fun all the same. Besides, you caught me."

He let her down and cleared his throat. "I guess I did. When we leave here could you, uh... Would you mind making it seem like you aren't coming with me of your own free will? The other goblins. They expect a kidnapping to be a little more dramatic than walking out with a mortal girl who's all too happy to leave."

She wasn't all too happy to leave. The world was wide and vast. That terrified her to the very bone.

But if they wanted dramatics, she supposed she could manage. Esther flipped her pale hair over her shoulder and nodded. "I can make a scene if I have to."

"Thank you so much." The words rushed out of him in a great gust of breath. "That will go a long way in making them believe I can actually do something right."

Her heart broke a little. This poor goblin boy just wanted someone to look at him and see a man rather than a child. Esther understood that.

So when they left her hut and walked toward the other goblins, she screamed like someone had cut off her toes. It was her best performance yet.

CHAPTER 4

*E*sther sat on a small cushion in the middle of a rickety cart across from Lux. She'd thought the faeries would travel some other way, but no. They rode in these horrible contraptions that were ready to fall into pieces. Every bump they hit made her worry that a side was going to fall off and leave her with her bottom in the dirt.

All the goblin wares surrounded her. A burlap sack the same size as Esther sat full of pomegranates and luxurious oranges. They'd stacked boxes full of crystals and jewels up to the cart's fabric ceiling that protected them from the rain.

She'd never thought to find herself here. At the very least, she'd expected that if she did find herself in a goblin cart, that it would be much more magical than shivering in the cold, damp corner on a cushion that smelled like mothballs.

Lux leaned over a box of diamonds and held out a

small nub of bread. "It's not much, but it'll keep you until we get to the Autumn Court."

Wasn't she supposed to avoid goblin food? That was one of the biggest warnings her mother had given her. If she ever found herself in the faerie realms, she wasn't to touch anything, eat, or drink. If she did, then she'd be stuck in that realm forever and never see her family again.

Some small part of her wondered if that's what happened to their parents. Maybe they had accidentally stepped into a faerie ring, didn't realize they were in the realm of the fae, and then ate something. It was a plausible concern, although Freya said that wasn't what happened. But Freya didn't know everything.

Esther took the bread and stuffed it into her mouth. "Thank you," she lisped around the food.

The goblin next to her shifted away with a slightly disgusted look. Was she offending the goblins around her with her horrible table manners? And here she was thinking just because she was with goblins, that meant she didn't have to be a lady.

Blushing, Esther knocked a few crumbs from the corner of her mouth. "Sorry."

"It's fine," Lux replied with a small smile. "We're all still learning from each other."

And apparently she was teaching the goblins that humans were gross creatures who barely knew how to eat without making a mess. Oh, she was making a fool of herself and she hadn't even the faintest idea how to recover.

Esther rubbed the back of her hand against her mouth for good measure, then asked, "Where are we going?"

"Faerie," the goblin next to her grumbled. "That's all you need to know."

Lux rolled his eyes. "We're going to the Autumn Court. That's where most of us goblins live. The other fae, they aren't..." He struggled to find the right word and then came up short.

She understood what he was getting at. She had always thought that faeries were beautiful, ethereal creatures who looked like gods and goddesses walking the earth. They should be otherworldly beauties who could convince the entire mortal race to bend a knee, if only they looked upon their perfect faces.

Such creatures were not goblins. They were ugly and grotesque. Their bodies were mashed together with animals and because of that, they looked more base. Lesser. Perhaps even more likely to be found on a farm than in a castle floating in the sky.

Esther thought it made them more endearing, however. She wouldn't know what to do with a godly creature that glowed in the sunlight.

Biting her lips, she sheepishly met Lux's gaze with a kind smile. "It sounds like a beautiful place to live. Autumn is my favorite season."

The boy lit up like she'd handed him a ring. "It is? It's always been my favorite, too!"

Every goblin in the cart groaned. The one next to her was the loudest, and she could almost feel his eyes roll.

31

He pointed to each of them. "You two are disgusting. You're supposed to be screaming and shouting because a goblin kidnapped you. And you aren't supposed to be making this any easier for her. Tradition is to kidnap, scare, and integrate into our society afterward. You're doing this all backward, Lux."

The unsaid words hung in the air. You never do anything right, Lux.

And if it didn't break her heart, that Lux leaned back into the coverings of the cart and tried to make himself small. He had been trying so hard, but he didn't have a mean bone in his body. He didn't want Esther to be afraid of her situation.

These goblins might know that tradition was one way, but Lux could look at the tradition and decide for himself if it was right or wrong. She respected that a lot more than someone who was willing to go along with what had always been done.

Esther stood up and wobbled over to Lux's side of the cart. They hit a particularly large bump, and she had to catch herself on the side of a box filled with emerald jewelry, but thankfully she didn't knock it over. Yet.

The goblins all leaned forward as one to catch anything that spilled, then leaned back into their seats with relieved sighs. "I'm fine," she muttered. "I'm not a child."

Esther plopped down beside Lux, crossed her arms over her chest, and glared at the other goblins. "So when are we getting to this Autumn Court, then?"

"Soon enough." The goblin she'd left glared at her. "And then you'll really be scared, little girl. Lux won't be able to protect you from the monsters that wait for you in the court."

Esther couldn't care less. They thought she'd be this terrified little mouse who hid behind the boxes of their jewelry, but she wasn't. She never would be. Her sister and parents had taught her to be so much more than a fainting daisy.

She muttered under her breath, "What kind of terrified people did these goblins kidnap before me? Monsters. Hmph. Goblins are just fae, and they aren't demons at all."

Lux shifted in the coverings. He lifted one red blanket away from his face and stared at her with those beady black eyes. "What kind of monsters would frighten you then? The fae are terrifying creatures. We can wield magic and fight in battles that would destroy the entire mortal realm. Not to mention we must look very odd to you."

"Perhaps. But there are stories of magnificent creatures that are so much bigger!" She tossed her hands up and launched into a story.

Esther loved telling stories, and Freya had never wanted to listen to her. She'd heard this one down on the docks as a child. The tale of a whale who was larger than three ships put together, with teeth the size of a man, and a thirst for mortal blood. She spun the story masterfully, and yes, embellished a lot more than the sailor's story. The web of her story laced around the goblins in the cart until they were all enthralled with her words.

"And then," she said, her voice deepened with emotion. "There was but one man left. A single captain clinging to the wreckage of his ship, legs dangling in the cold salt water."

Lux's eyes had widened so much she worried they might pop out of his skull. "The captain was the only one left? No one in the crew survived?"

"No. A captain goes down with his ship, so it's an even worse story." She took a deep, dramatic breath and then sighed sadly. "As he stayed in those waters, the whale circled him below. He kept waiting for the moment when its mouth would open wide and swallow him like it had all the other men on his ship. But it didn't. The monster whale waited until another ship saw the man floating in the sea. Then it turned to a new battle and feasted again."

A goblin with fluffy white rabbit ears on his head twitched them one by one. "So you're trying to say that this whale was smart enough to use the old captain as bait?"

"Well, a monster that large couldn't be satisfied with a single ship full of men. It's just not enough meat." At least, that's what the sailor had told her all those years ago. She'd been just a little girl, and her father had been so angry that she'd heard the story.

Esther will have nightmares for weeks, her father had claimed. Instead, her head had been full of seafaring adventures and monsters from the deep. She'd never been afraid of the story. Only interested in hearing more.

She'd collected stories her entire life. And considering the way the goblins were all staring at her with wide eyes and mouths slightly open, that would help her in the long run. They were interested in stories as well, particularly ones from the mortal realm that they might not have heard yet.

Lux took a deep breath. Tiny wrinkles appeared in between his brows as he leaned back against the cart wall and chewed on his lip. "Well, that's an interesting story. But I don't think any of us would be afraid of a whale. Even one as large as that."

Her temper flared. She'd just told them all the most magical, intense story she knew and all they could think of was that they had experienced more terrifying things than that? Then a whale that rose from the depths and swallowed entire ships because it had a taste for mortal blood?

The other goblins chuckled at Lux's words. A few even muttered agreements as the cart slowed.

They were making fun of her, weren't they? The adorable little mortal girl thought she knew what scary was, but had yet to experience the true terror lurking in the faerie realm. Well, they could try to scare her. But she refused to feel fear.

Lux held out his hand as the cart rolled to a stop. "Esther, allow me to be the first to introduce you to the Autumn Court."

That sounded better than sitting in this cart with these miscreants. After all, just how scary could a court of faeries be? Her mother used to claim it was a never ending dance of magical folk and powerful creatures. Esther was certain she already knew what to expect.

So, she ignored his outstretched hand and waltzed to the end of the cart by herself. "I don't know why you're all so insistent on trying to scare me. Nothing could be in the

Autumn Court that is more terrifying than living in the mortal realm. Shame on all of you."

Without a thought, she opened the flap of a door and dropped to the ground. She'd already seen goblins, for heaven's sake. What more could she see?

A crowd of people waited to help unload the cart she'd been in. But these weren't people at all. A man with the head of a cat hissed at her and lunged away as if she might try to grab him. A woman with an owl's head twisted her skull all the way around to stare at Esther with unblinking eyes. All around her were people that shouldn't exist. Humans stitched together with beasts like some demented doctor had sewn together the beings he wanted to exist. Like a madman had stepped into the shoes of God.

She gulped and pressed herself against the cart, returning their wide-eyed stares with one of her own.

"H-Hello," she stuttered.

Another goblin rounded the cart at the same time as Esther's travel companions started pouring out. Esther recognized this other goblin for a brief moment. He'd been the elderly one on the white horse. The one she was certain had kept the others in line.

But then he threw off his cloak and suddenly, he was another man. One with molten silver skin and eyes that flashed with galaxies. He drew himself up tall and proud, cracking his neck with a flourish that sent his dark hair spilling over his shoulders in a shadowy waterfall. "Horace! Thank you for inviting me to go with the little ones. I forgot how fun a Goblin Market is."

"It was a pleasure, my King." Horace dropped into a

low bow. "And now we deal with the mortal who's returned with us."

The Goblin King grinned at Esther, sharp teeth flashing in the dim light. "Good luck. I have a feeling I'll be dealing with her sister in only a moment's time. Until then, we'll see just how brave these mortal women are."

CHAPTER 5

*E*sther would have stayed frozen against the cart for hours if they let her. And not entirely because the creatures here were terrifying. They weren't that bad once she got used to staring at them. But also because the court itself was stunning.

This land was aptly named. Every inch of the forest seemed caught in a suspended version of autumn. The leaves were bright red and orange, falling from the trees in a never-ending cycle like rain. Deep leaf piles covered the ground and her skirts swished through them even when the wind wasn't blowing too hard.

Lux ushered her off to a tree nearby and tucked her into the nook of the roots. "Stay here," he muttered. "We have to get everything unloaded and then I'll return for you."

Esther might have once argued with him and tried her very best to cause trouble. But right now, she wanted to watch these half human, half animal people unload a king's ransom of jewelry from the cart. Over and over they handed boxes that seemed to be pulled out of the depths Esther didn't remember traveling with. Each box was loaded with more impressive jewelry than the last.

Diamonds. Emeralds. Sapphires. She couldn't fathom where they had gotten all these precious gemstones or why it was goblins that had them. But they were beautiful. So intensely beautiful that she daydreamed about draping herself in all the necklaces and bracelets until Lux came back for her.

The rat-faced boy wrung his hands together and watched her with a narrowed gaze. "We're done. I'm supposed to bring you back home now."

Home?

Esther supposed that made sense. He was the one who had kidnapped her, although he still hadn't explained why that was any sort of tradition. And she supposed if any of the goblins were going to bring her home, she'd rather it be this sweet young man who still turned bright red whenever she looked at him.

Scrambling up from the ground, she nodded. "All right, then. Where is your home?"

"Uhh..." He scratched the back of his neck and that embarrassed blush spread down his neck. "How comfortable are you with heights?"

"I used to climb trees when I was a little girl." She frowned. Why would knowing how she was with heights matter?

"Good." He held out his hand for her to take, waggling his fingers. "Come with me."

She knew the words weren't meant with any romantic intent. He wanted to get her to his home so he could figure out their next steps. But there was something so sweet about him. Something so endearing that it made her entire chest squeeze tight.

Esther slipped her fingers into his with a soft smile. "Heights, huh?"

"Heights." He repeated. Then Lux drew her away from the tree and into the forest beyond.

All the tree trunks were beautiful here, too. Esther hadn't realized she could think a tree was beautiful, but she was proven wrong by the forest they walked through. Every tree was more stunning than the last. Silver birches with bright yellow leaves. Golden oaks that rained leaves like fire on the ground.

Sure, she should have been afraid here. A strange goblin boy led her through a forest, a journey that could end in her doom. Esther hadn't the faintest idea what goblins did to the mortals they made deals with. But how was she supposed to be afraid when the world here was so captivating?

Everywhere she looked was filled with color and echoed with sound. Birds sang from the tree tops and strange goblin creatures moved through the golden light that never seemed to fade. This was a magical place full of magical people, and she never wanted to leave.

Never wanted to leave? What a curious thought.

"Here we are," Lux said.

She focused on his bright red face and realized the poor boy was embarrassed yet again. As if he didn't want her to see where he lived. She wondered why.

Esther looked around for a door or even a small hut, but there wasn't one. Instead, all she could find was a small ladder made of rope and wooden planks. Following it up, she saw it led all the way to a treehouse nestled between the branches of a rather large red oak.

The treehouse was very similar to something she and her sister would have built with their father. The roof was awkwardly slanted, and the siding wasn't even. Not even close, but it was still quaint and adorable.

She only had one worry. Clearing her throat, she glanced over at Lux and said, "I thought it would be a little bigger. But that's all right. I hope we're good at sharing small spaces."

"I think you'll be surprised." He clambered up the ladder and shouted, "Come on then! It's not much, but it's home from now on."

Right. She needed to climb the ladder and then clarify all of this situation. After all, what was home? What was she supposed to do in this faerie realm when he had kidnapped her and brought her here? Obviously there was some sort of expectation for those who made goblin deals. Esther just wasn't aware what that expectation was or what it might turn into.

The wooden slats were worn and sanded. She barely even noticed they were wood because someone had made them so smooth. All the way she clambered to the top of the small ladder where Lux waited for her with his hand outstretched.

As she stared up at him, sunlight beamed behind his head. It illuminated the beautiful coloring of his hair and skin. Almost as though an angel was reaching for her. She couldn't bear to think of him as a demon, even with those odd looks. His face was too kind. And besides, who said angels had to be beautiful? Or at least conventionally so.

Esther grabbed his outstretched hand. He yanked her up from the ladder and for a single moment she hovered in the air. Nothing but him holding onto her.

Breathless, she stumbled into his arms within the treehouse. Her palms pressed against solid muscle and muscular biceps. She'd thought this boy was wiry, but instead, she held onto a rather strong young man.

"Oh," she whispered, staring into his dark eyes.

Lux mumbled something that sounded a lot like a very long, "Hm", before releasing her and taking a step back. He touched a hand to his heart and rubbed furiously. "Well, this is my home. It's not much but..."

Apparently he didn't know what else to tack onto that thought. It wasn't much. That was all he thought about the place where he rested his head every night. Poor dear.

Esther looked around and realized he was very, very wrong. The treehouse was much larger inside than out. Bright, colorful swaths of fabric covered the walls like tapestries that weren't sewn yet. Reds, blues, and yellows spread out before her eyes in luxurious vibrancy. A few pillows were strewn about the floor for people to sit on. In the back corner was the smallest kitchen she'd ever seen. She'd never been all that fond of cooking, anyway. Two large tree branches broke through the walls behind the kitchen, but there appeared to be two rooms in the back.

The rat-faced boy walked a little closer to those rooms and pointed. "Bedroom to the left. Bathroom to the right.

It's all aided by magic, so if you need anything that isn't there, you can just ask the tree. It'll... You know."

She didn't. She had no idea what a tree would do if she asked it to do something for her. Would a tree even know what she wanted if she asked for lavender soap?

There were so many questions boiling in her head, but Esther didn't know which one to start with. Did she ask about their journey? This home? Magic? The fae?

Finally, what burbled out of her mouth was, "You've kidnapped me, so what's next?"

The goblin boy stared at her, dumbfounded by her question that he obviously didn't know how to answer. "Uh... What do you mean?"

"Well, the other goblins said there were rules to being kidnapped by a goblin. You even said that I had to scream when we arrived at the cart, and I did that with all the grace of an actress." She was quite proud of her performance, and he hadn't even complimented her on that. "So what's next?"

His eyes widened with every word. Almost as though he didn't know what to say to her when she asked such things. And that made worry churn in her belly.

"You don't know what's next, do you?" she asked.

"No." Lux shook his head and swallowed hard. "No one talked to me about the next steps. They said to take you here, because goblin brides are always stolen, and then... Well, that's where they stopped telling me what to do."

The words stuck in her head. Two simple words that rolled over and over until she whispered, "Goblin bride?"

The terrifying goblin had said the same thing, but Esther had thought she'd misheard him.

"Oh." He pressed his hands to his mouth and shook his head. "You didn't know that part? Why don't humans know anything about our traditions?"

He appeared angry that he had to be the one to explain this to her, but what did he expect? She hadn't even known buying something from the goblins would curse her, let alone send her off into the wilds of the faerie realms.

Esther planted her hands on her hips and glared at him with every ounce of anger running through her veins. "Obviously not. I heard one of the other goblins say something about a goblin bride as well. What does any of that mean? I thought you were just going to kidnap me?"

"I should have confirmed you knew."

"You think?" she screamed the words while wildly waving her hands over her head. "And you still haven't explained what the hell any of this means! Goblin bride. Lux, tell me what that means or I'm going to lose my mind!"

He gulped and took a step back toward the bedroom. "Maybe I should let you calm down before we talk about this. It's a tough conversation to have, you know?"

Every ounce of her sister channeled through her body. Normally, Esther was the nice one. The calm one. She could talk through any situation and no one would know she was even angry. But this was an entirely uncommon situation.

She pointed at the goblin boy and ground between her teeth, "You stop moving right now, Lux. You will tell me what is going on, or I will rip that tail off your body and make you chew on it until you finally give in."

He gulped again. "You're terrifying. You know that, right?"

"Good. You should be afraid of me. You sold a necklace to a young woman who had no idea what that meant. It looks just like the necklace my mother used to wear, which can only mean you know something about her, or where she is." Esther took an aggressive step forward. "I refuse to believe our meeting was just by chance. I want to know what you know. And you should be afraid because I am a woman without family or friends here in this realm. I will do whatever it takes to get what I want."

He swallowed hard again. "Unfortunately, that will be difficult. By goblin law, we're now married."

All the blood drained from her face. "And what does that mean to goblins?"

"Well... Just that we're married. And like you said, there's no one else here for you. So I'd imagine you'd want to be a bit kinder to the only person who can help you." He shifted his direction toward a window. "Besides, haven't you ever heard you catch more flies with honey?"

"I don't want to catch any flies, that sounds like a horrible infestation to welcome into your home." She crossed her arms over her chest and gave him an unimpressed stare. "Are you going to hop out that window?"

"I'm not running away from you, if that's what you're asking." He darted to the open window, threw a leg over the sill, and then saluted her in the strangest chain of events she'd ever seen. "But I think it would be smarter if both of us had time to cool off. I'll be back! House, don't let her out."

He dropped out of sight and Esther let out a snarl. He'd left her all alone in a strange place, in a magical treehouse, with no one but her thoughts to keep her company.

"Damned goblins," she muttered. "Worthless. The lot of them."

CHAPTER 6

*S*he stayed in that little room for as long as she could stand it. Sure, that wasn't very long in the grand scheme of things. Maybe a day, probably shorter if she was being honest with herself. But if he wanted her to stay where she was, then he should have said so.

What kind of man climbed out a window when something happened that he was uncomfortable with? Esther had wanted to have a proper conversation with this goblin boy who seemed to think he didn't have to tell her what was going on. It was her life. Esther knew she had a very compelling right to know what was going to happen to her. And yet, he still climbed out the window, one spindly leg after the other, and left her alone in this treehouse.

For a whole day.

No, it was far too much for her to handle. Esther was in the faerie realm for the very first time in her life. She had to explore.

The front door wasn't letting her out, though. She had

tried it many times, thinking perhaps it had something to do with the position of the sun. It wasn't. That goblin boy was smarter than she'd thought, because he had certainly cast a spell that locked her into his treehouse home.

The window was looking more realistic with every moment. Esther walked over to the goblin boy's escape hatch and peered down. They were very high up and she wasn't sure she'd survive that jump. But if she couldn't, how did he?

It wasn't like rats were good at landing on their feet. If he'd had cat whiskers or a cat tail, she might have thought he would have some other magic that allowed him to land on his feet. But he wasn't.

She placed her hands on the windowsill and leaned farther out. Freya would have screamed at her to not take risks like that. As the wind blew over her face and shoved at her shoulders, Esther allowed herself to feel a little more free than the second before. No one was here to tell her what to do. Her life was completely and utterly her own.

Even to risk.

And if she hadn't leaned out of the window like she did, then she never would have seen the plush bed of autumn leaves waiting for her on the ground. The pile was thick and lush, obviously meant to catch someone if they plummeted from the treehouse.

It was the escape she needed. Perhaps the goblin boy wasn't as smart as she'd given him credit for, then. He should have hidden that if he wanted to keep her in the treehouse while he was gone.

Esther gathered her skirts up and clambered onto the

ledge of the window. She popped her butt down on it and looked over her shoulder for a second glance at the room she was leaving behind. It really was a cute little home that he'd created for himself. She hoped that someday she might return.

Without another thought, she slid from the treehouse and tumbled down toward the bed of leaves.

The wind stole the very breath from her lungs. Esther clenched her jaw, so she didn't let out a yell that would warn all the goblins where she was, but then she landed rather quickly. As suspected, the leaves prevented her from harming herself, but they didn't stop the air from whooshing out of her lungs.

Wheezing, she took some time to breathe deeply. Goodness. Maybe that wasn't meant to be as easy as she'd thought.

Esther rolled onto her hands and knees, then dragged herself out of the red and orange leaves. Many of them stuck in her curls and even more had somehow shoved down into her bodice. She tugged handfuls out while wandering away from the treehouse.

Which way did she want to go?

Left was the way they'd come. That way would lead her toward more goblins, so she should probably not go in that direction.

Right had a road that meandered into the trees beyond. Roads usually ended with people as well, so she didn't want to go that way either.

All that left was going straight ahead into the thicker copse of trees that disappeared into a black forest. Perfect. Esther had strode confidently through forests her entire life. This time wouldn't be any different.

The leaves fell from the trees, sprinkling onto her head. Esther stared up at the golden leaves that looked as though the deft hand of an artist gilded their edges. This place was more than just a forest. Magic lived in every fiber of this place. Every leaf wasn't just a mortal leaf, it was a faerie leaf. Every single vein glowed with power and magic.

Esther hadn't realized just how beautiful the faerie realms would be. Her mother always warned that the realms showed whatever temptation would call out to the human that wandered over the thick carpet of leaves. But Esther didn't think that was correct now that she was here. This forest was beautiful, yes, but it wasn't exactly how she would have built it. Instead, this place was designed for itself.

Sometimes, she could hear a breath when she walked. And not the sound of another person breathing or trailing along behind her. The hairs on the back of her neck would have stood up if someone was watching her. No, this was the breath of the forest itself.

The trees made the sound every time the wind brushed through their leaves, and yet another shower of color rained down on her shoulders. Esther's entire soul seemed to light up with every step. Her heart screamed this was where she was meant to be. Perhaps just this moment, wandering through the woods, or maybe this was the land where her soul could finally feel at home.

Branches crunched underneath her feet and snapped her mind out of its wandering path. Before her was a giant pool of water, green with algae and dotted with lily pads that lay flat on the surface. She might have taken the time to bathe if a face didn't appear out of the water.

Or not quite a face, really. The elongated head looked like that of a horse, although the fur was bright green and blended into the algae blooms just below the surface. Its nostrils flared and the horse within the water snorted, blowing in her direction as though it wanted her attention.

Oh dear. Esther couldn't remember any species of faerie that lived in pools of water. And she knew her mother had talked about them.

Why hadn't she listened more as a child? Her mother had always made it seem very important that her daughters were aware of every possible faerie creature that might try to harm them. But Esther's mind went blank the moment she needed to know what creature this was.

So far, everyone here had been kind, though. Maybe this one was just like the goblins.

After all, her mother had said a goblin deal would lead only to her own demise. And look at where it had gotten her? Esther now lived in the faerie realms and wandered about wherever she wanted to go.

"Hello," she said hesitantly. "I'm sorry if I disturbed you. I've only recently come to the faerie realm, and I'm afraid I don't know the rules very well yet. If this is your land, I apologize."

The beast rose out of the water and Esther gulped. It wasn't a horse at all. Though its back legs were equine, its front limbs were the muscular and bulging arms of a man. The faerie creature planted its hands on the side of the pool, fingers flexing in the muck, before he met her gaze with a smile. The lips stretched over pointed teeth that no horse would ever have. "Don't apologize, little mortal. Very rarely am I visited by one of your kind."

She had a feeling that was for a good reason. This beast looked eerily familiar, but her heart was thudding so hard in her chest that her mind couldn't think around the sound.

Polite. Be polite, that's what her mother had always said. If she found herself around a faerie that she didn't know, the very least she could do was be polite. Faeries valued respect over everything else.

Esther dipped into a low curtsey, holding out her dress with both hands and hoping there weren't too many leaves in her hair. "It's an honor. What are you doing in this pool, though? Don't you have a home somewhere else?"

"This is my home, mortal child." The beast leaned down onto his elbows, for it had to be a him, and sank into the water with his back half. "You don't recognize what I am, do you?"

"I don't." Her face flamed with embarrassment. "I know that I should, for my mother was very thorough in my teachings."

"But you didn't listen to her, did you?" He tilted his head to the side, teeth flashing again. "Good. I like that in a lady. You shouldn't listen to what everyone else says, my dear. Your opinions should be made in your own time. Meet the faeries that your mother hated. See what you think for yourself."

Esther had thought the same thing. Her mother was

always been so afraid of their kind, to a point of hatred. Freya had followed in their mother's footsteps and couldn't be swayed, no matter how many times Esther tried to convince her that maybe there were good people among the fae.

She snapped her fingers and pointed at the faerie. "That's exactly what I used to tell my mother! But she didn't think that was very smart. She said all faeries were the same, even if I wanted to believe there was more to their kind."

"What a sad way to look at life." He dug his fingers into the mud, inching closer to her. "Well, I'm a kelpie if you were curious."

Kelpie. She'd heard that term before, and it was one of the fae her mother used to warn her about the most. These creatures were known to steal women to the bottom of their pools, drowning them so they could feast on their flesh. Although some kelpies wanted a bride as well. Their children were abominations incapable of feeling anything other than anger or rage.

Maybe her mother had been wrong about that as well. This faerie didn't seem to want anything from her other than her attention. Perhaps he was lonely and wanted someone to talk with. Esther knew she would be lonely if she'd been in the forest by herself for a very long time.

"Well, then." She took a step closer to him and smiled. "My mother used to say your kind killed more mortals than any other. She said you convince young women and men to fall into your pool of water and then you devour them whole."

"Oh, never whole." The kelpie's grin somehow widened even farther, so much so that all his gums showed bright red and glistening. "We like to pick them apart, slowly. I'm a fan of sucking out the meat from inside your bones. That's the tastiest piece, you understand."

Esther stared in shock because certainly she'd heard him wrong. He couldn't be talking about sucking the marrow from her bones when she had just given him the benefit of the doubt? He was a faerie, like the others, and he must not want to be a monster. A killer. A devourer of mortal women who were unfortunate enough to fall into his home.

Esther was so surprised, she'd frozen in place. Even though she could see the kelpie lunging toward her, that mouth opening wide and all those teeth gnashing. But she had been so certain that she wasn't wrong. That this beast couldn't want to hurt her when she had known...

Well, she hadn't known. She should have listened to her mother and to Freya, who were right all along. There were faeries who were dangerous and wanted to hurt her. Esther had just ignored them because she so desperately wanted some of them to be kind.

Strong arms wrapped around her waist and whipped her out of the kelpie's path. The band of muscle and sinew would leave bruises, but she couldn't bring herself to care. She was safe in these arms, even though she loathed being saved.

Lux breathed out a long sigh in her ear, and the sound was one of complete and utter frustration. "What are you doing?" he snarled. "Playing with kelpies on your first day here isn't the smartest choice."

"I wasn't playing with him," she whispered in response, but she could hardly hear her own voice over the pounding of her heart.

The kelpie grumbled and slid back into the waters of his pool, eyes glowing red as they sank beneath the turbulent waves. She could still feel him watching her long after the glowing lights of his eyes faded beneath the dark water.

"I didn't think he would hurt me," she said. Esther leaned her weight against Lux, incapable of standing even though she'd managed just fine moments ago. "He seemed kind. He said he wasn't like the others, or maybe that's all I heard... I just... I just..."

She didn't want him to be mad at her. For all that she had done, Esther wanted Lux to see something more than just a foolish mortal girl in her. After all, they were apparently married by goblin law. And the last thing she wanted was for yet another person to be disappointed in her.

Lux sighed but tucked her underneath his chin all the same. "You're all right, Esther. This was my fault. I shouldn't have left you alone and not expected you to escape. You aren't like the other mortal women I've met. You're brave, and foolish, and yes, you don't see faeries the way others do. I should have known you'd want to explore."

The words weren't fair to him. He was taking all the blame when she was the one who had run out into the wilderness and gotten herself nearly eaten. Esther pushed out of his arms and shook her head. "No. This was my fault. But I'm afraid. I don't know what's dangerous here, and what's not. I don't know why I'm here, or what I'm supposed to do."

Was she hyperventilating? It felt like it.

But this was always her problem. Esther thought she knew what was happening or even how to be a good person, and then the rug was ripped out from under her. Her thoughts were wrong. Her experiences were odd. Everything made little sense, and how was she supposed to learn from this? To grow? Was the lesson that everything was dangerous, and yet again she had made the wrong impression of these fae creatures?

Lux reached for her hands and squeezed them tight in his. Those dark eyes filled with some emotion she couldn't name, but that eased the tension in her chest. "Esther, we'll get through this together. I brought you to this realm and I won't let you suffer for too long within it. Do you understand?"

Ah, there was the fresh air she needed. It flowed through her lungs as though his words were a sip of cool water. "Yes, I do."

"Good. Now perhaps we don't let you wander on your own anymore. That means you're coming with me." He released her hands and rubbed the back of his neck. "Which, ah... I guess that also means you're going to see more of the faerie realm than you might be ready for."

What Lux couldn't know was that Esther was ready for all of it. Even when the terror was still clutching her heart, she knew without a doubt that she wanted to see everything this goblin boy offered.

CHAPTER 7

*L*ux took a while to prepare for their journey. Apparently, there was a lot more for him to pack now that she was going with him. Esther allowed him freedom for multiple days until she finally forced him to sit down across from her.

With a sharp shove of her hip, she knocked him onto one of the chairs and stood in front of him, forcing him to remain in one place for long enough to listen. "Lux, stop moving. I have questions."

He blinked up at her like he didn't know what she was saying, and then finally the haze lifted from his eyes. "You have questions?" he repeated.

"A lot of them, actually." Esther didn't know how to verbalize all of them yet, but he had a few things that he needed to answer before they went anywhere. "But first, what do you know about goblin brides? I need to know that."

He twisted his hands in his lap and the sigh that erupted from his chest was enough for her to know what he was going to say. "I know nothing about goblin brides. It's not like that's a normal thing for goblins to run around kidnapping. Most of the time, people who make deals with us are just... well. They're nobility, normally, and they're already married. And they make an actual deal. They aren't buying something because it looks like a necklace their mother wore."

Yet again, she was the outlier to the normal. Esther supposed that was just going to be how she spent the rest of her life. Always a little different from everyone else. Even the fae.

She pursed her lips and tried to think of a way around this. "Wouldn't someone here know what's expected then? If we're married in the eyes of all the goblins, I want to know more about all of this. Am I supposed to be a wife to you? Is there a ceremony? Where's my ring?"

A ring seemed very mortal of her to want, but Esther had always assumed things would go a certain way for her when she was finally married. There would be a proposal, of course. A beautiful proposal full of magic and starlight and a man on his knees who begged her to love him.

The usual things that every girl wanted from the man she loved.

But Esther didn't love this rat boy. She hardly even knew him, although she would give him the benefit of the doubt because he seemed like a kind-hearted young man and he had been very good at saving her thus far. But that didn't mean he would make a suitable partner, or that she could ever bring herself to love a man with a rat tail.

"Hm." She hummed out the sound long and low

when he didn't respond to her. "Are you going to answer any of these questions or no?"

His eyes got even wider, and he shook his head. "Probably not."

"Really?"

"Really." He shrugged helplessly. "Your guess is as good as mine in answer to any of those things. As far as I can tell, we're on our own. No one has taken a goblin bride in a very long time, and realistically, most probably brought them here and then tucked them away in a cabin in the woods. A kelpie would get them, but then at least the mortal woman was out of the goblin's hands."

"Why would they want that?" Esther had a hard time believing that was what they all wanted. To get rid of their mortal brides. Why would they make a deal if they didn't want to be around her kind?

Lux wiggled his way out of the chair and stood up. "Most goblins don't want a mortal running around and getting into things. You're all notoriously difficult to keep an eye on, and most mortals don't like the faerie realm to begin with."

"Oh." She swallowed hard and stepped away from him. "Is that what you're going to do then?"

It hurt to think he'd want to throw her away like that. Even though she'd already had a few missteps, that didn't mean she was ready to give up the opportunity to explore. To see everything that was so close to her grasp.

How frustrating. She wanted to see all the magic, but needed his permission to do so. It just didn't seem fair for him to have that much control over her life.

Small furrows appeared on Lux's brow. He shook his

head with a slight tsk. "I don't know who convinced you that leaving was the only option in your life, but I don't want to throw you away, Esther. I want you to be more careful, that's for certain. And I'd appreciate it if you listened to what I have to say, because I know a lot more about this realm than you do. But I'm not like other goblins. I took you on as a bride, and I mean to treat you like a real one."

Because he was a good man.

She'd forgotten that to his very core, Lux had proven time and time again that his intentions were pure. His soul shone with so much goodness and light that it was nearly blinding.

Sighing, she pressed her hand against her chest and tried to lighten the moment. "Good! I do believe I'd follow you around like a puppy if you tried to leave me somewhere all by myself. I'd be most difficult to deal with."

He snorted. "Now that, I believe."

They smiled at each other and she felt something click in her chest. As though her heart had been a locked box and he'd just opened it with a skeleton key that she hadn't known existed. He smiled at her and the entire world lit up underneath her feet. She wanted to hold him. Hug him. Draw him to her breast and never let him go.

He cleared his throat and pointed behind him. "Besides, we're all packed now. Finally. The Goblin King himself chose a few people to go on missions around the Autumn Court and uh... Well. I was chosen. So I guess that means you're coming with me."

"Missions?" That sounded rather ominous. She felt her heart beat faster and adrenaline rush through her veins. "Are we going somewhere dangerous? Are we sneaking into a castle and stealing some magical object the Goblin King wants?"

Lux smiled softly, as though he didn't want to encourage her strange behavior, but also as though he enjoyed every word she said. "No, nothing like that. You'll see once we get going. The Goblin King is rarely the person to instigate war, you'll find. He's more interested in bettering all the kingdoms at the same time. It's a bit more complicated than someone like me can understand, but I trust the man."

Well, that was less exciting. Esther tried very hard not to pout too hard as Lux gathered up their things and handed her a pack.

She grabbed it and almost immediately dropped the whole thing onto the ground. This bag weighed as much as her!

"What did you put in this?" she grumbled.

"All the things we need to bring. Come on." He held out his hand for her to take. "We're traveling by portal."

"Portal?" Was that magic? Of course it was. That was a foolish thought to even think.

Esther let him drag her from the treehouse, down the ladder, and out into a small clearing covered in red and orange leaves. He reached into his own bag and pulled out what looked very much like a harmonica.

"Here we are," he muttered, holding it up to the light. "Hold tight to me. Portals are notoriously finicky. If you let go, I can't promise we'll end up in the same place."

"That's a portal?" She frowned, trying very hard to see how a harmonica was going to take them anywhere. "It's an instrument."

And a boring one at that. There weren't even inscriptions on the metal sides. It was just a bronze harmonica that had seen better days, and some of the smaller pieces inside were already rusted. She wasn't sure it would even make a sound if Lux blew into it.

He shrugged. "Magic doesn't need to be tied to something functional. I found this on my very first trip to the mortal realm, and I've had it ever since."

"It was a portal in the mortal realm?" She frowned even harder, scrunching her entire face in concentration. "Did a witch make it then?"

Lux laughed and wrapped an arm around her shoulders. "Look at you with all the questions. No, Esther. It didn't have magic when I found it. I'm the one that enchanted it to take me where I wanted to go, and witches aren't real."

"They absolutely are." She'd met a few in her lifetime and no one could explain their magic away. They were real. That's why her mother had ushered Esther away from them so quickly.

"Right, you can believe that all you want." He snorted. "Humans with magic. All right then, you hold tight to me and we're off. Ready?"

She didn't want to get lost after some shoddy magic sent her careening through a portal and back into a kelpie pond. With her luck, it would shred her first and then throw her limbs all over the place. With that fear running through her head, she grabbed onto Lux for dear life and squeezed her eyes shut as hard as she could.

The sound of the harmonica was the first warning that he'd already cast the spell for them to fly out into the magical world. Then she heard wind whistling through her ears, but she couldn't feel it on her face or whipping through her hair. In fact, she really didn't feel much of anything until the very last second when they struck the ground so hard her knees cracked.

"Ow," she muttered. "That hurt."

"I didn't say portal traveling was easy," Lux replied with a chuckle. "Now, follow me. The King sent us here because a lot of the inhabitants of this town are out of work. A mine nearby collapsed, and that was their only way of making anything to trade. They don't have as many jewelers here, but they're trying to train up the most talented artists they have, and then they'll send some of their younglings with us the next time we go to the mortal realm."

He said the entire story flippantly, as though it were something she should recognize and know. But Esther didn't understand any of what he said.

"Send them with you?" she asked, even though her own voice sounded dumb to her ears. "I guess I'm not really understanding all this."

"Goblins make their money through jewelry, or in the making of it. We're the ones who bring it to the mortals so we can get something in return." He pointed over his shoulder toward the looming buildings. "They're the ones who get the metal for us. They collect it from the earth, casting the right spells for respect so the court doesn't rise up and eat us. That sort of thing."

Oh, right. That sort of thing.

Esther held her tongue still and wandered after him, lost in her own thoughts. The town they headed toward had seen better days. The buildings were little more than small shacks with brightly colored roofs that now were dotted with the dark shadows of holes. Goblins left their homes and trailed out into the sunlight as soon as they got there.

Each goblin was more strange than the last. They were all part animal, some with patches of worn fur and others with scales. All of them looked at her with curious expressions, but then turned their attention to Lux and Lux alone.

As they approached him, Esther noted how sunken their cheeks were. Not a single goblin who walked toward them was overweight. Most of them were little more than skin and bone, wandering across the leaves of their home like skeletons shambling toward their next meal.

The first goblin reached Lux and held out her hands. She had the sunken features of an owl who was moments from death. "The King sent you?"

"He did, matron." Lux leaned down and pressed his thin lips to her fingers. "He asked me to extend his deepest apologies that it took so long for us to get to you."

"There were others who needed more." The owl looked past him and her gaze caught on Esther, standing awkwardly behind them. "And who is this? The King didn't mention a mortal woman coming with you."

Esther hardly thought the Goblin King expected her

to be traveling along with Lux on this mission. And she probably looked like something Lux had gathered up off the forest floor somewhere. The heavy pack on her back made her entire body bow into its weight, so she appeared to be a hag who had traveled through the wood hoping to find some unsuspecting mortal to prey upon.

Sighing, Esther waved. "Hello. Mortal woman here."

"Yes." The owl frowned and looked back at Lux. "I can see that."

To his credit, Lux didn't seem interested in telling anyone anything about Esther. Instead, he pulled his own pack off and set it on the ground. "I'll explain later. But first, let's get your people fed, shall we?"

The owl woman couldn't argue with him. She snapped her fingers and most of the other goblins rushed forward. Lux spent the rest of the afternoon reaching into his pack and pulling out more food than ever could have fit in the small space. Maybe that's why they were so heavy.

Esther had placed her own bag next to his, but he never reached for the other one. He left hers completely untouched, and that was when she knew they had more villages to go to. More people to help save.

He looked up at her once with a twinkle in his eyes and grinned. "Was this what you thought we were going to be doing?"

"Not at all." Esther curled up on the ground near him, wrapped her arms around her knees, and watched as he spoke with each and every goblin.

Lux took care of them. Better than most. He didn't care that they were dirty or starving. Instead, he treated every person who approached him exactly the same. He handed them food with a smile and a soft sound of encouragement, most he even called out by name. She'd never seen someone as dedicated to helping others as this rat-faced goblin boy.

She squeezed her arms tighter around her legs. The more she was around her new husband, the more she realized how lucky she was.

How many mortal women were married to a man like this? A man who genuinely wanted to help others and then did so?

She didn't know how long she sat there watching him, but eventually he finished and turned to her with a bright grin on his face. "You watch long enough to get a hang of it?"

"What do you mean?"

He held up the harmonica and then pointed to her pack. "We've got a few more stops on our journey, Miss Esther. I thought maybe the next one you might want to help pass everything out. Since you're so interested in goblins, that is."

She bounded to her feet, gathered their things, and reached for his waist. "You read my mind. I'd like nothing more than to help."

The grin on his face widened even farther, and he blew into the harmonica while staring into her eyes.

CHAPTER 8

*E*sther was used to working hard. She'd spent her entire life subjected to garden labor with Freya beside her, both of them sweating until the sun went down. But that hadn't prepared her at all for a day like this.

Her back hurt worse than when she was bent over spending the day weeding in the garden. Her neck felt like she'd whipped it around too fast, and tiny tingles spread down her spine every time she looked to her right. Even her fingers hurt. How, she wasn't sure, but the joints in them screamed every time she made a fist.

But she'd also never felt so fulfilled in her life.

Those goblins had really appreciated all the help she'd offered. Sure, the food wasn't hers. But she had assisted in giving it out. She'd carried some of the food back to individual homes and put it all away because the goblins were too weak to do it on their own. Esther had even gotten a pot of soup going for one of the elderly goblins who had ears like a basset hound. The woman had pressed a single gold coin into her palm, saying they had no need for metal when food was about.

She would do this a thousand times over again in her life if Lux would let her. Esther's heart exploded with the sensation of doing so much good in such a short amount of time.

This was what she'd been missing in her life. The chance to do something more than just work for herself. Freya was always so concerned with their own needs, that she'd never looked beyond. Never thought about the ways they could help other people.

Esther bit into the sandwich Lux had thrown together with a satisfied moan. "I had no idea food could be so good."

"It's a lot better when you've worked for it, that's for sure." He grinned, mouth full of chewed up bread with a small piece of lettuce hanging out of his mouth. "You did good today, Esther. Worked harder than a lot of mortals I've met before."

"I've worked hard before," she replied with a chuckle. "I just thought gardening or working in the woods would be harder than handing out food. I was wrong."

"Surprising how it sneaks up on you, isn't it?" He took another hefty bite of his sandwich and let out a little sound of happiness of his own. "You know, I thought when they told me that I had to take a goblin bride, that I would have to endure a ridiculous amount of boredom. Most mortal women expect a house and a safe place to rest their head at night. And yet, here you are after a hard day's work and we'll be sleeping under the stars. You haven't complained a bit."

She'd never been one for complaining, if she was being honest with herself. Complaining meant that she wouldn't have enough time to get the job done, and once someone asked Esther to do something, she would complete it. Even if that took her a hundred days to do.

Face bright red, she tucked a strand of hair behind her ear and chuckled. "I guess I haven't. But really, there has been little to complain about. We're helping people. I don't care if that's hard work."

"I'd think you find there's many people who would disagree with you on that. Hard work is hard work. No matter who you help." A shadow passed in front of his expression, before he smiled at her again. Gesturing at her with his sandwich, he asked her a question that sounded very serious. "Something's bothered me since I took you from your home, though. You were all too happy to leave that place. I was always told mortal women screamed and cried, but you? You wanted to leave."

She supposed she had. But how did one say that even though they were living in a loving home with a supportive family, that they'd still felt trapped?

Esther knew he deserved the truth of it, though. And really, she'd told no one how she felt about Freya or her family, or even the little cabin on the edge of the woods. She'd held this dark, horrible secret to her chest for so long now that it felt as though the darkness was part of her.

It would be nice to let it out for once.

So she took a deep breath, swallowed hard, and let the words fly off her lips. "I don't think anyone in my family or village knew me. I lived with them my entire life and they all felt too comfortable telling me who and what I should be. But I didn't want to hate the things they hated. I didn't want to live the way they lived. And no matter how many times I told them that, they said I'd grow out of it. I'd be a different person once I was older. All the usual things that people say when they don't want to hear your opinions."

Even her sister.

And Esther loved Freya more than anything. Little Esther had thought her sister was a magical being. All she had wanted was to be strong and confident like Freya, but then she got older and realized that her sister wasn't strong or brave. She was just afraid.

Everything that was "other" scared Freya to her very core. And those odd, strange, unusual things inspired Esther to want to see more of them.

"Ah," Lux said quietly. "So you didn't see eye to eye with your family."

"That's a way to say it." She set her sandwich down onto the makeshift plate he'd made out of a very large leaf and sighed. "She doesn't want to see the world in a better light, and I don't want to see reason. No matter what we talked about, my sister and I would inevitably disagree on the very fundamental things in life. She wants me to grow up. I want her to realize that I have and this is who I am now."

"It can be hard to tell a sibling that you're no longer a child." He winced and then rubbed his jaw as if remembering a time when it had been struck. "Trust me, I know that very well from experience. Listen, family doesn't have to always like your choices, but they do have to support them. And if your family isn't supporting what you want to do, what your soul is calling you to do, then they don't have to be your family anymore."

Esther scoffed at the mere thought of cutting her sister out of her life. "She's blood, Lux. She's the only sister I'll ever have. I can't just cut her out of my life completely, that would be foolish."

Wouldn't it?

Her sister had helped raise her. Hell, Freya had given up her own future to make sure that her little sister was well taken care of and always had food on the table. Without Freya after their parents had mysteriously disappeared, Esther would have been left to some other family member who wouldn't have given her anywhere near as much love or attention.

Esther owed Freya a great debt. She just didn't know what that was yet.

Lux watched all the thoughts play across her features with rapt attention. And when she had finally concluded that she was indebted, he shook his head in disappointment. "Listen to me, Esther, and listen well. Just because someone shares your blood doesn't mean they have the best intentions for you. Everyone is looking out for themselves first and foremost. It's life. But those that don't serve you, who don't improve your life... They shouldn't get to be in your life at all."

Well, that was food for thought.

Esther didn't think Freya made her life worse for wear. If anything, Freya had made it easier for Esther to become this version of herself. She'd provided the safe place for Esther's mind and opinions to grow on her own, regardless that her sister didn't agree with them.

But what if she was wrong? What if, like the kelpie, Freya hadn't wanted to support her decisions at all?

Now her mind was all in a muddle. She'd left because it had felt like the right thing to do. Esther was notoriously bad at decision making. She didn't think about what she was doing, she just acted. If she wanted to leave, that's what she did. The consequences would and could be dealt with later on.

She hadn't thought about the fear her sister must feel right now. She hadn't expected to feel guilty for leaving without even letting Freya know where she'd gone, or that she wasn't in any horrible danger. Esther had left without a word, swanning about her life without a care for anyone else's feelings. And yes, that was where she got hung up.

"Adventure," she whispered. "That's all I ever wanted. I wanted to feel like I was exploring the world and all the things in it. But a life with Freya wasn't doing that. I would have died in that little cabin with my sister at my side, and we never would have experienced a single part of the world."

"Why's that?" He seemed genuinely interested in her answer, and for that she was grateful.

"I suppose Freya is terrified of the unknown. Just like our mother was. Just like our father let them be." She scratched her arm and tried to convince herself it wasn't that bad. She hadn't left her sister in a fearful situation where all her nightmares had been unveiled in one fell swoop. "She'll be all right, though. Freya's the strong one."

"I'd say you're both very strong," Lux replied. "Look at you. You're in the faerie realm without a single worry in your head, helping goblins like they don't scare you one mite."

"They don't," she replied with a smile. "You all think you're so terrifying, but you really aren't."

She'd heard far too many goblins ask why she wasn't scared of them. Sure, maybe there were some humans out there who would have screamed just looking at a goblin. They were odd to stare at, and some of their pupils were slanted sideways like a goat's. But that didn't matter to her. They were all very polite beings, and they seemed welcoming of a young mortal woman who was impeding on their home and even their happiness. They were good people. That's all that mattered to Esther.

"Hm," Lux hummed low in his throat. "You see? Brave, after all. I don't know a single young woman who would come into the Autumn Court and help all of us. And I certainly don't know many women who would leave their families behind without worrying about what would become of them."

"I do worry about all that," she corrected. "I just don't talk about it that much, I suppose."

"Or you don't let it bother you in the end. Either way, you're an impressive young woman, Miss Esther. And I'm lucky to have met you." His face turned beet red. "I shouldn't have said that."

Electricity zinged down her spine. He thought he was lucky to have met her? She supposed she had been very helpful today, but that wasn't what he meant. The heat of his gaze swept her from the top of her head to the bottom of her toes, then dashed away like he'd done something unforgivable.

Could she think of him as a proper husband? He was a goblin. He had a rat tail, for heaven's sake. But when she looked at him now, Esther had a hard time seeing the rat boy any longer. He was hardly a goblin in her eyes. Just a young man who had a heart of gold and who looked at her like she'd hung the moon in the sky just for him.

She swallowed hard, then cleared her throat. Suddenly she was so very parched. How had he done that to her?

"Ah, well." She cleared her throat again. Why couldn't she speak like a normal person right now? Now that he was paying attention to her as she wanted him to. And, at the same time, she didn't want him to look at her like that at all.

Again, he grinned. Lux reached for a stick and poked the fire with it. "I never thought I'd find a mortal woman beautiful, you know. You're all so... pale and worm-like."

That snapped her right out of her stupor. "Worm-like?" she repeated, aghast that he would compare her to something that crawled through the dirt.

"Well, yes. Look at you! Goblins are all textures. We have fur, scales, and feathers. Our kind are meant to look like something the earth made on a whim and spat out in the hopes that we'd look all right. But your kind? You're all smooth. Like river stones that were tumbled too long in a current." The grin on his face didn't budge for a moment.

Esther thought he might be teasing her. Trying to get her to feel a little better about being called ugly by the man who was supposed to be her husband.

She crossed her arms over her chest and glared at him. "Oh, really? Well, how might I make myself more beautiful to you, goblin husband of mine?"

"You'll get there." He shook his head ruefully. "Magic touches everything in this place. Eventually, I'm sure you'll find yourself to be just as beautiful as the most wild of goblin women."

The implication there was terrifying. Did he mean she was going to turn into a monster just by living here? Esther realized very quickly she didn't have it in her to ask for further clarification. She wanted the conversation to return to their light hearted banter from before.

She changed the subject back to the strangeness of his form. She talked about how mortal men looked without their shirts, because she used to spy on them when they were bathing in the nearby creek, and watched Lux's expression turn from teasing to horror.

She'd ask him about the magic, eventually. But for now, she wanted to flirt with her goblin husband and feel her chest turn all mushy every time he told her how beautiful she was. How her laughter made his chest light up like a bonfire.

And it was good. Every second with him felt like a lifetime of happiness.

CHAPTER 9

*S*he had just finished giving out the rest of the food in her pack and let the other goblins in her line know that they needed to go see Lux. He had more left than her. He'd taken to using her bag for most of the villages they went to, because her back was hurting from carrying it even in the short amounts of time they needed to go from each town.

Her heart broke at the realization that the goblins didn't seem disappointed or mad she'd run out. Instead, they all smiled at her and nodded. Like they understood there was only so much to go around, and even if Lux didn't have enough for them, they were just happy that some people in their village got to eat.

These goblins never stopped shocking her with how easy going they were. Sure, she knew if there were a war, the goblins would be the worst sort of people to battle. But for now? They were lovely. Wonderful and kind.

"Excuse me, Miss?" A hand tugged on her skirt.

Her initial reaction was to warn the poor dear away

from touching her at all. Esther hadn't bathed in quite some time, and the clothes she wore were the same ones she had started traveling in. Unfortunately, these did not smell good at all.

But then she looked down into the sweetest, heart-shaped face framed by giant rabbit ears that brushed the little boy's chubby cheeks. The white fluffy additions to his head looked so soft that she wanted to stroke them.

In his hand, he held out a small red flower for her to take. "This is for you," he whispered, his cheeks bright red. "Thank you for bringing us food. We really needed it."

"I'm just here with Lux," she replied. But she still took the flower. How could she not?

He had clearly mustered all his courage to bring her the tiny gift. And it meant more than she thought it would.

Esther tucked the bloom behind her ear and grinned. "How do I look?"

"B-b-beautiful," the little boy stuttered before bolting away from her. He ran to his mother, who was waiting in line with Lux, and Esther couldn't quite get the grin off her face. She was making baby steps towards these people, not just appreciating her, but genuinely liking her. She was turning this court into a home, and she hadn't been all that sure it would be possible.

Lux finished up in another hour and found her where she had curled up in the roots of a tree. Esther had taken to wandering off a small distance to watch the faeries as they went around their home. Goblins were fascinating creatures, and they didn't mind if she watched them go about their daily business.

He sat down next to her with a slight groan, then pointed to the flower in her hair. "I see I have competition for your attentions."

Esther touched a finger to the red flower and her cheeks burned. "He's just a child. But he is quite adorable, so you'd better watch out."

"Really? How curious. I hadn't thought a little boy could beat me, but apparently I've been rather disappointing."

Oh, he's been anything but disappointing. Every day she watched him with the other goblins, and it made her heart squeeze tighter and tighter until she didn't know what to do with it. Would it eventually explode in her chest and then spew words out of her mouth that she couldn't take back?

Goodness, she was going to end up being one of those horrible romance novels her sister used to hide from her. Wasn't she? She'd gotten all twisted up inside over this goblin boy she didn't know, and nothing was going to stop her heart from claiming him as her own.

They were married, after all, and if she wanted him, then she supposed she had every right to have him.

Esther managed a laugh and hoped she hadn't missed anything in the conversation while she'd been wandering through her thoughts. "I don't think a child could steal me away from you, realistically. He's a very adorable little man, though. I'm impressed with his bravery."

"Bravery?" Lux lifted a brow and met her gaze with a curious frown.

"Well, it's not easy to walk up to a girl you might like and give her a gift. Even a flower has meaning. The perfect gift is a choice that should take a very long time to figure out." She supposed, at least. Maybe she'd read a few of her sister's romance novels and that had given her some ideas about romance.

It wasn't like Esther had the time to figure out romance on her own! She'd never had a boy interested enough to hold her hand, let alone bring her gifts or come to their small cabin in the woods and hope Freya would let him through the door. The townsfolk had always whispered that she and her sister were more likely to be witches than anything else. That led to a certain amount of fear and, yes, loathing.

But if she had to hazard a guess, she would assume that the correct gift had a lot of meaning to the young man who was choosing it. And if the gift was wrong, then the young woman had every opportunity to not accept the gift.

Where would the boy be then?

She was digging far too deep into her own thoughts again and had no idea if Lux was even sitting next to her anymore. Sheepishly, she met his gaze again and bit her lip. "Sorry, did you say something?"

"I didn't say a word. I've gotten rather used to you meandering through your own thoughts. I can always tell when you're away with the faeries." He reached out and tucked a strand of hair behind her ear. "Besides, that's all right if you want to think for a while. I'm never going to interrupt a conversation, even if it's with yourself."

Away with the faeries. She hadn't ever heard of that

one before, but she liked it. That's a bit what it felt like when she wandered sometimes. It was hard for her to focus on one person for too long, let alone think about their emotions until the doing was already done.

"Well, I'm here now," she replied. "Sorry for wandering again, but if you wanted to say something, then I'll listen now."

"Ah, good." He clapped his hands to his legs and stood up. "I also have a gift for you, although I'm not sure if you'll like mine more or the pretty flower behind your ear. Either way, I'd like you to come with me and see what I've found, if you're willing."

She would always be willing to go with him, no matter what he wanted to do. Or where he wanted to take her. The mere idea that he'd thought about her enough to get her a gift? It sent her heart fluttering again.

Lux held his hand out for her to take, and she imagined that he was offering something much more than just an adventure for the afternoon. She imagined he wanted to spend the time with her because he'd missed her all day. That even though they hadn't been that far from each other, he had wanted nothing more than to be by her side.

Eyes wide, heart in her throat, she reached up and took his hand. He drew her up to her feet with effortless strength, and the grin on his face was the answer to every question she'd ever had in her life. Everything would be fine. He was here.

She trailed along behind him through the forest. Leaves crunched underneath her feet and the scent of earth and crisp air filled her lungs. She could breathe here so much better than in the mortal realm, though she didn't understand why. It was like the air itself was filled with electricity that traveled throughout her entire body every time she inhaled. The magic of this place fueled her.

Eventually Lux stretched out a hand, palm flat and fingers spread. He was warning her to stop, although she didn't know why they needed to be hesitant. Esther remembered what he'd said about her trusting him.

So, she didn't ask her questions of why they were stopping. Instead, she froze in place and held her breath.

Lux lowered onto the ground, stretching out his body until he had to crawl through the leaves. He motioned for her to do the same. Together, they quietly slid over the ground and made their way up a tiny rise. It was a small crater, she realized. The earth turned sharp and steep just over the lip of this hill and dipped down to a large pool of water in the center. There, a kelpie stood in the water, its large belly heaving as it searched the water with its snout.

"I thought you said they were dangerous?" she whispered, still a little nervous to be around a kelpie considering what had happened the last time she'd seen one. Didn't he remember the horrible nature of that beast who had tried to drag her into the water?

Maybe she hadn't dealt with the memories of her near death experience very well, now that she was thinking about it. That faerie had proven her wrong on every single thing she'd thought she knew. Faeries could be dangerous. Her mother and Freya hadn't been lying.

But this kelpie wasn't looking at them. Her greenish fur was matted around her head, the mane on the back of her neck tangled with seaweed. And her sides were moving like the poor thing was hurt.

Her heart twisted and did that awful flip again. She might be afraid of the beast, but she didn't want it to be in pain. Nothing deserved to hurt like that.

She looked over at Lux and saw that his eyes had a misty sheen to them. "What?"

"You fought through the fear of this beast right in front of me, and I'm proud of you for doing that. Is all." He cleared his throat and turned back to look at the kelpie. "She's pregnant, and kinder than most. I thought you'd be interested in seeing what that looks like, considering your great fear of them. I thought it would be helpful for you to see them as more than just monsters who lurk beneath the depth, but... Well you already fought through that fear on your own."

She supposed she had. Esther didn't enjoy holding onto any emotion that didn't serve her well. She could toss fear to the wind if the opportunity was right for her to do so.

"Oh," she breathed. "I suppose this is a much better gift than a flower then."

"Is it?"

Esther couldn't think of a better gift. He'd wanted to make sure that she was more comfortable in her new home. And he hadn't known what else to give her, other than a way for her to conquer her own fear.

He'd proven that his greatest desire was to see her happy in the faerie realm and that... Well, that was captivating.

No one had done that for her before. Freya had

wanted Esther to be happy, but she'd never asked her sister what would actually do that. Freya was more the type to give Esther what she thought would suit, and if it didn't, then Freya refused to understand why Esther couldn't be satisfied with the same things that met Freya's needs.

Lux was the first person to think of Esther as an individual. To get her what she wanted rather than what everyone said, she should want.

Oh goodness. There was that awkward flip in her chest where her heart stopped beating because he was looking at her with those dark eyes and all thoughts leaked out of her ears.

"Yes," she whispered. "It's perfect."

And then she leaned forward, pressed her lips against his, and hoped this was the right way to kiss. After all, she'd kissed no one else before, other than practicing on her hand after she'd seen someone do it at the market.

The desire in her chest to kiss him had been too much to deny. She had to kiss him. She had to do something that would show him just how much it meant to her that he saw her as a person and not as something to be controlled or tamed.

Lux wanted her to be happy.

And she was. Esther was so incandescently happy that she couldn't think when she was around him. She had to act.

His arm curved around her shoulders, drawing her closer to him with every breath. Eventually she stretched out over his chest, kissing him until there was no breath in her lungs that didn't come from his. And she wouldn't have it any other way.

He kissed her as though she were water and he a man who had found himself in a desert. Esther didn't stop him from devouring her lips and tongue. How could she? She hadn't realized this was what kissing would be like. She'd thought it a strange thing for men and women to press their mouths together, but she hadn't realized it could feel like this.

Like her soul was peeling away from her body and drawing nearer to him. Like her heart pounded in her chest for him and him alone.

Every fiber of her being drew closer to him. This strange goblin boy with his arms around her shoulders and his hand stroking her back.

No, not his hand. She drew back from his kiss with a soft laugh and peered over her shoulder to see his tail had wrapped around them as well. A tail. She should have shuddered in revulsion but she could only think about how sweet it was that he'd lost his head so thoroughly that he'd touched her with something that he usually tried to hide.

Although, she'd admit, the tail wasn't that bad now that he stroked her spine with it.

"Sorry," he muttered. Lux scooped his hand under her jaw and drew her attention back to him. He followed the sharp edge down to her chin where he pressed a soft kiss to her skin. "I can move it if you don't like it."

"No," she replied, shaking her head. "I don't want you to move it."

His gaze heated again, and Esther knew that was the

right thing to say. She wasn't frightened by it at all, and in the end, she liked that he felt comfortable being his complete self with her.

Esther sank back into his arms and they spent the afternoon learning each other's taste and the feeling of their hands stroking over shoulders and backs. Esther didn't let it go too far, although she might have. Maybe. She didn't know what would happen if she let him continue to draw the shoulder of her dress down.

She finally felt like they were husband and wife. Even if that was just kissing him.

And she could kiss him forever. Without question.

CHAPTER 10

*E*sther lost track of how many goblin villages they traveled to. Every few days the packs they carried filled with food, water, and sometimes blankets or clothing. She never knew what she was going to get when she opened up the pack. But it always matched with whatever the particular village needed.

Eventually, they ran out of people to help after about a month of traveling throughout the entire Autumn Court.

"We're done," Lux said as he joined her after a particularly difficult village needed their attention all day. "This was the last one."

"Good," she moaned. Esther flopped down onto the ground and let her arms fall to the sides. "I think my entire body needs a bath. Or a massage. Or maybe just to sleep for eight days in a row. I'm not sure yet."

He stood over and grinned down at her prone form. "Ah, there's the complaining. And here I was thinking you didn't know how to complain at all. You were starting to seem more magical than a goblin, Miss Esther."

"At some point, everyone is going to complain. I'm exhausted," she said, but a grin spread across her own features as well. "I wouldn't change a single day of our journey, though. These people needed our help, and we did the right thing by helping them. I'm sure of that."

He held out a hand for her to take, then hauled her up onto her feet. "Bravo, my dear. Bravo. Now, we can enjoy ourselves if you'd like. This particular village always has a festival each year to celebrate the harvest. It'll be a bare bone one, of course, but there's always dancing and an enormous bonfire. It might be a good way to reward ourselves for all this hard work."

Honestly, she wanted to go to bed. But he had such a bright look in his eyes that she couldn't tell him no. He wanted to do this, and she would do anything to keep him this happy.

She took his hand, let him help her to her feet, and then followed him through the village to the center where the goblins were already placing wood in a large circle.

The goblins had pulled out all the fabric from their homes. Blankets hung from tall poles that they slowly lifted into place around the fire pit. There would be beautiful colors surrounding the bonfire and whipping in the wind. Esther knew they would make this place delightful in a matter of seconds if they wanted.

A lizard goblin with a long tail lashing behind it strode toward the fire with a great torch in his hand. He lifted it above his head, whispering words of magic that made no sense to Esther, then plunged the torch onto the piled wood. It burst into bright flames that danced with a hundred different shades of red, orange, and yellow. The magic had given it a life of its own and a rainbow to throw on the fabric they'd hung.

Quickly, the goblins dragged other items out of their homes. Chairs, pillows, more blankets, anything that could be used as something to sit on and ease the ache of the ancient bones of the older goblin men and women. The younger goblins emerged from their homes with instruments in their hands. Although, they weren't the ones that Esther was expecting.

She would have thought violins and cellos, the normal instruments for dances in the mortal realm. Esther had only been to two in her life, the few that her parents had taken her to. That had all stopped when they disappeared because Freya didn't want them to go to the festivities within the village. She thought they were unnecessary.

The goblins apparently weren't at all like the mortals. They held in their hands trumpets, drums, even a few harmonicas like Lux had as a portal. All these instruments looked like they would create a horrible sound that would haunt Esther for the rest of her life. But when they lifted their musical choices to their lips, and lifted their drum sticks, they created a rhythmic beat that called out to something wild in Esther's chest.

Maybe she was wrong, then. The goblins seemed to know much better what music would bring a soul to dance, rather than the stuffy strings she was used to in the mortal realm.

"Do you want to dance?" Lux asked, with a wry smile on his face.

"Do you know how?" Esther lifted a single brow and watched him with a rather skeptical expression on her face. Intentionally, of course. She could tell just by looking at him that he'd be an incredible dancer.

She couldn't help herself in that she had to tease him. He deserved a bit of ribbing for all the work he'd put her through.

Though she would admit, her body felt better than it had in ages. Working in the fields or on their small cabin didn't have the same effect as what they'd been doing lately. She was so tired at night that she hardly had time to even think about the fact that she'd left Freya in the cabin by herself.

Esther was glad of that, though. She didn't want to think about the horrible way she'd left her sister. And she didn't want to acknowledge the guilt that was gnawing through her belly at any given moment.

"I know how to dance," Lux replied, his voice cutting through her guilt. "The question is whether or not you can keep up with a goblin. In case you didn't notice, our dances aren't like yours."

"No, they aren't. I wouldn't expect the goblins to dance anything like mortals." She hoped they didn't. Esther strode into his waiting arms and placed her hands on his shoulders. "In fact, I'm hoping that this dance will differ greatly from what I expect from such festivities. I want to see what you can do, Lux."

"Then allow me."

He spun her into a dance that was wild and free. He

whirled her around the fire, joining in the crowd of goblins that whooped and shouted with voices of man, woman, and beast. He called out his own trilling response with an expression of complete and utter abandon.

She lost her breath in the wildly spinning steps he guided her through. But she lost her heart when she saw how genuinely joyful he was. She didn't know when it happened, but she had lost her heart to this mad goblin boy.

What was she supposed to do now? She couldn't tell him how she felt. He had married her because of something she'd done, after all. Esther was the one who had trapped them both in this arrangement. And though they were both enjoying their time together, that didn't mean she hadn't trapped him.

What if he was just making the best of a bad situation? She wouldn't be surprised. Esther wasn't good at recognizing situations like that. She assumed everyone liked her until she realized they were just indulging her oddities.

Lux whirled her again, reaching down, putting his hands firmly on her waist. He lifted her up over his head and all the thoughts drained from her mind. He liked her too. She was certain of it.

Even when she looked at him with a smile on her face, his shoulders straightened like she'd given him a gift that no one could take away. When she tilted her head back in the dance and laughed, his hands clutched her a little closer. As if he didn't want to let her go any time soon, but also wanted to see what would happen if he spun her out of his arms and into the crowd of goblins.

The drum beats spread through her, mimicking the rapid thuds of her own heart. Every step, every sway, every twirl, they all fell in line with the music that became the sound of her own soul.

And when they were too breathless to keep dancing, Lux drew her away from the crowd. They stood at the very edge, holding hands and trying to catch their breath around the laughter that neither of them could stop.

"Well?" he asked. "Can I dance after all, mortal bride of mine?"

"I suppose you can," she replied. Keeping her cards close to her chest seemed to be the best situation right now. Esther didn't want him to know how she felt just yet. The words felt like they would ruin this moment. "Once I catch my breath, I intend on convincing you to teach me the correct steps. I'm not really sure what I'm doing out there."

"No one does. A goblin dance doesn't have steps. It's just the music of your soul leaving your body in movements that you cannot control."

Oh, she quite liked that. What a wonderful way to describe dancing when so many others had tried to make it stiff and forceful.

Lux grinned at her again and reached for her hand. "We have little time before the next part, though. Goblins have a particular way of ending a festival like this. Usually only couples do it, and if they succeed, then they guarantee a year of happiness in their relationship. Will you try this with me?"

Her stomach rolled. "What is it?"

"You just have to trust me, my dear. Can you do that?"

She didn't know, but so far, she'd done so with no issues. She supposed she didn't have any choice. Blowing out a long breath, Esther squeezed his fingers in hers and nodded. "Yes, of course."

They rushed back into the pack of goblins that Lux pushed through. The goblins parted like a wave until Esther and Lux stood in front of the bonfire once again. He looked into her eyes and asked one more time, "Do you trust me?"

The flames reflected in his eyes, but not in a frightening way. All she saw in those eyes was a level of passion that she could only hope to reciprocate someday.

Esther nodded firmly. "Yes. I do."

That wild look in his eyes burned even hotter. He tugged her arm hard and darted toward the fire. Though she might have hesitated for the briefest of moments, Esther reminded herself that she'd said she trusted him. And if he wanted to rush into a bonfire, then she had to trust he wasn't doing it to set them both ablaze.

Lux leapt into the air and tugged her with him. A magical wind pushed underneath her feet, almost as though someone had reached for her heels and threw her straight up in the air. That weightless moment wasn't spent alone, though. She watched Lux as his tail whipped behind him, solidly keeping him in the right direction and ensuring not a single lick of flames touched Esther. Not one.

They landed hard on the other side, rolling over the ground and into each other's arms. He held her close to his chest, making sure no stones bruised her skin. And when they tumbled to a stop, Lux rolled to keep her on top of him. Just as they had when they stared down at that kelpie.

His eyes were wide and his mouth curved into the softest of smiles. Lux reached up and tunneled his hands into her hair. "You're beautiful," he whispered. "And I never thought I'd say that about a mortal woman."

"Oh, would you stop saying that?" she whispered, leaning down to kiss him with all the hope and love in her heart. "We both know I'm not entirely human, and that's why you wanted to make a deal with me in the first place."

Though she was distracted by his kisses, her words range in her head.

She wasn't entirely human. Or maybe she just didn't want to be anymore.

The words wouldn't go away, no matter how hard she tried to dash them from her mind. And in that moment, Esther knew nothing would ever be the same again. The truth was right there for her to grasp.

She wasn't human anymore.

CHAPTER 11

The words never left Esther's head. She didn't get a wink of sleep, even after a night of dancing and partying with the goblins. Wine made her head spin until she swore she could hear the phrase whispered in her ears.

She wasn't human.

She wasn't meant to be a mortal woman anymore, and that's why she'd found the goblins. Her life had taken twists and turns that couldn't be contained by a life in a cabin by the woods.

The only way to accept this was to change herself. She needed to recognize that this form wasn't the one she was meant to be in. The only logical next steps was that she had to find out how to become a goblin.

Obviously, there was only one person she could ask. Lux.

Though there was the bitter taste of guilt on her tongue because she knew Freya wouldn't like this. But her sister wasn't here right now, and Freya hated the fae, anyway. She couldn't understand the need deep in Esther's chest that called out for her to do the one thing that felt right.

Changing herself permanently was a big step, but one that was going in the right direction. Esther didn't question this choice in the slightest.

Lux had just finished packing everything they would need to bring back with them. He wasn't happy to return to his portion of the Autumn Court, she could see that in the way he moved. Every now and then he'd kick a rock or some dust. His shoulders were rounded, and he blew out long sighs every time someone brought him a gift to return with. Although, she had thought those gifts might cheer him up.

Instead, he looked very much like he was going to vomit at the mere idea of returning to his home.

Hopefully that would work in her favor.

Esther walked up behind him and put a hand on his shoulder. "Lux?"

"I'm fine," he muttered before realizing who was talking to him. At the sight of her, he lit up. "Esther!"

"I know you aren't excited to go home," she whispered, stepping close to him so none of the other goblins would hear them talking. "I just don't understand why. I like your treehouse. You've built a lovely retreat for the times when the Goblin King doesn't send you on a wild chase throughout the court to help everyone in your path."

She'd thought it a funny thing to say, but he didn't take her words the right way. If anything, Lux only grew more morose.

"Whenever I go back there, I return to the same boy I've always been my entire life. The rat boy who is too young to do anything right. The Goblin King sees that I'm useful, that's why he sends me out to gather information or help when I can. But those missions are few and far between. No one there sees me as useful."

The words struck her to the very core. Esther forgot how similar they were in their lives and in their frustrations.

She stepped into his arms and wrapped her own around his waist. Squeezing him tight, she pressed her lips to his collarbone. "I think you're brilliant. I see all the work you put in for everyone around here and even in your own home. It's a shame they don't see what I do, but at least you'll have me now."

He hugged her back. "I appreciate the kind words, Esther, but we don't really know each other at all. I stole you away from your family, and there's still the chance for you to realize that you want to go back. And if you did..."

He didn't have to say the words. She already knew how he would finish that sentence if he could.

Lux would bring her back to the mortal realm if only she asked. Cruel men would keep a woman with them, even when they didn't want to be. But he wasn't a cruel man. The honor running through his veins would insist that he bring her back to her home so she could be happy. He'd deliver her with an apology, likely some kind of pie for Freya to eat, and then she would never see him again.

The mere idea caused a shiver to run down her spine. She didn't want to say goodbye to him. Not now, not ever.

"That's what I was hoping to talk to you about." She leaned back in his arms and stared up into his curious eyes. The dark gaze usually saw right through her, but Esther realized he did not know what she was about to say.

He was afraid. Fear shivered through his entire body because he was so scared she wanted to leave after all. That he would return home alone, yet again, just the rat boy that no one wanted around.

"Oh goodness, no, not that." She shook her head and cupped his jaw in her hand. "Lux, the exact opposite of what you're thinking is what I want. I want to stay here forever, with you. And I don't want the chance to return to the mortal realm. I feel very much like I have a foot in two worlds that are pulling me in too many directions. All I want is to stay here. All I want is to be like you. A goblin."

"The magic doesn't work like that," he muttered. "You'd have to be here for a hundred years to see the effects. So many people leave here. You've even met some of them. Those witches you claim are real are usually people who lived in fae for a while and then returned when they grew bored with their faerie lover."

"Well, I'm not like them. I don't want to be one of those strange women with powers no one can explain. I want to be half woman, half beast." Esther grinned at the mere idea. Maybe she'd end up with feathers in her hair and delicate bones that let her float in the wind. "I want you to look at me and think that I'm beautiful, not despite being mortal, but because I'm one of your own kind. That's what I want."

His eyes widened with every word until he stared at her like she'd lost her mind. "You want to turn into a goblin?"

"Yes." Esther nodded. "And you will not change my mind. I want to be a goblin, and I think this is the best choice for the both of us. As a goblin woman, you'd have a real wife. And you'd never worry that I would want to go home, because they would kill me if I returned looking like a goblin."

He shook his head in denial. "And you? What do you get out of turning into one of us? It's not as magical as you seem to think, Esther."

"I get to stay with you." The words rocked through her entire body, pressing against her soul where she felt it finally take flight into the air. "I get to live in the place where I'm finally happy. I get to see you every single day and know that without question, I made the decision that makes my very soul lighter than a feather."

He licked his lips and the furrow on his brow deepened. "You can't go back from this. If you want to change back into a mortal, there's no way for me to do that. You'll be stuck as a goblin for eternity."

"Then let's be goblins together. We'll frighten little children in their sleep and sell necklaces made of gold and silver to unsuspecting nobles." Esther released her hold on him and danced back. She raised her arms from her sides and gave a little spin. "No one will know what kind of monster we are, but you and I will be happier than any person ever has been in their life."

He watched her dance, and the anxiety disappeared from his expression. She could see the understanding dawning in the expression of awe on his face. "You really want this, don't you?"

"Yes. More than anything I want to be just like you." Esther stopped spinning, her heart racing and her mind in a tumble because she was so sure he had been ready to tell her no. "And you know how to turn me into a goblin forever, don't you?"

"I do. But it won't be easy."

She didn't care if it was difficult. Impossible was the word she feared more than difficult. Esther knew how to overcome hardship, and it was easier than most people thought. All one had to be was dogged in the intent to get what they desired.

And Esther had never desired anything more in her life than to be with him for all eternity.

Lux stepped away from her, leaving their packs behind. He tucked his hands behind his back, then circled her and the packs. "Magic is something that cannot be controlled as easily as most humans think. Namely, magic isn't singularly owned by the person who is wielding it."

She felt very much like she had walked into a school room. Apparently, this was to be her very first lesson on becoming a goblin.

She mimicked his posture and tucked her own hands behind her back. If it made her look more serious, then so be it. "You'll have to explain a little better than that, I'm afraid."

"Ah, well." He frowned and took a little while to figure out how to say what he was going to say. Then he continued. "The magic that I use to cast spells is the same magic that the Goblin King himself uses. It's not coming from me or him. It's coming from a central source that is everywhere. There is a certain place we can all look for it, where it tends to pool more than other places, that is."

She was following so far. "So what you're implying is that we need to go to this centralized location of magic and that's where I can turn into a goblin?"

"Yes and no." He scratched the back of his neck. "We won't be doing it at that point. I can't enter the well."

"Oh."

So that was why he was so nervous. Not only would she be agreeing to change her form, but she would have to do this on her own. He wouldn't be able to help guide her once she got to this magical place. Esther would have to keep her resolve all on her own, and she wouldn't be able to change her mind. Or if she did, it would be a lot more difficult to do so.

But would she? She already knew that this was what she wanted. She didn't plan to change her mind halfway through this process, namely because she didn't think she would be happier as a human.

After all the thoughts ran through her mind, and after she decided her own opinion, Esther nodded. "All right, then. That doesn't change my mind, Lux. If I have to walk alone and perform whatever ceremony it requires on my own, then I'm fine doing that. I will do it gladly."

"There's no ceremony. Just asking the magic to give you a gift in the form of becoming a goblin."

She could do that. Esther wasn't great at asking for anything from anyone, but she knew that if push came to shove, she'd be able to verbalize this desire. Besides, asking magic for something was like whispering into a wishing well. And she'd done that many times in her life, even if those wells weren't really wishing wells in the mortal realm.

"I want to do this," she replied. "I know it might seem like I haven't thought it through, or that I don't really know what I'm doing, but I do. My entire life has been plagued with people asking if I ever thought any action through. Well, this one I did. I've thought about it a lot and every time I come to the same conclusion. I want to become a goblin, and I want to stay with you for the rest of my life."

Lux appeared surprised at her speech, but he straightened and squared his shoulders. "All right, then. Leave the packs. We'll get them later. It's time to turn you into a goblin."

And if her stomach twisted with more than a little sadness at leaving her entire family behind, Esther refused to acknowledge the feeling.

CHAPTER 12

"*A*ll right, listen carefully." Lux crouched behind a nearby tree and gestured for her to stoop down with him.

He'd spent the better portion of a day arguing that she would want to run back to her home eventually, and wouldn't that be easier if she didn't go through with this?

Esther's answer never changed. She would not run home to see Freya. She definitely would not change her mind any time soon. And if he didn't want to support her through this mad plan, then that was fine, but she would find someone else to take her to this pool of magical water.

That shut him up pretty quick. Once he had the same answer enough times, Lux finally let it go. Which meant they were able to focus on the task at hand, which was getting her into the temple where the water was kept.

Of course it was in a guarded temple. They couldn't let just anyone walk into the temple and steal from their power.

She'd thought it would be easier than this. If someone wanted to become a goblin, why wouldn't the others just let them?

Whatever. This wasn't her land, not her rules, and she couldn't control any of the goblins. If they didn't want people around their temple of magic water, even though the only people who would be around it were other goblins, then she supposed they had every right to put guards at every corner.

Scrunching down onto the ground beside him, she ducked her head low so no one would see her next to him. "I'm listening."

"There will be three guards out front. There are a lot more guards ready to hop through portals at any moment. And when I mean a lot, I mean close to a hundred of our very best warriors. They are not who we want to see." Lux gulped at the thought of these powerful creatures arriving. "Do you hear me?"

Esther had to control herself so she didn't roll her eyes. Did he think she didn't hear him? Really? She was crouched in the dirt with her ear practically pressed to his mouth. Of course she heard every word he was saying. "Understood. Do not rile the guards. Don't get anyone else called. What else should I know before walking in there?"

The leaves shifted beneath his leg as though he had tensed at her words. "You are not going to walk in there without a care in the world. I'm not kidding when I say those goblins would sooner kill you than they would let you walk through their beloved temple. So you are going to sneak in quietly while I lure them away."

"And just how are you going to do that?"

He shrugged. "Probably by throwing a couple stones in the bushes. The farther away they are from the entrance, the more likely you are going to be able to sneak by them. I think it will be fine."

Hadn't he just said these were the most powerful warriors in their kingdom and that getting any of them involved would end in certain death?

Esther frowned. "What if you get caught? You won't be doing anything wrong, I suppose, but you certainly won't be allowed to stay."

"They won't do anything if I get caught. Like you said, I'm not in the temple itself. And everyone knows I'm just a boy who likes to prank people. If they see me, they'll know who I am and let me go." He gulped. "I hope."

"I don't want you to take any unnecessary risks for me either. There may be another way for us to accomplish this." Esther placed her hand on his in the dirt. "There has to be another way, and if this is too risky for either of us to do..."

"It's not." Lux shook his head in denial and flipped his hand over. He intertwined their fingers, and she knew everything was going to be okay, just like he said. "When I go, you go. Understood?"

Of course it was understood. But suddenly her stomach was flip flopping and the meager dinner they had pressed against her throat. Esther rarely worried for herself. She had a knack for getting out of situations that she shouldn't be in. But Lux? These were his people. And if they were caught, then he was the one who would suffer the worse punishment.

Just before they focused on getting into the temple, Lux reached out and caught her face in his hands. He stroked his thumbs over the high peaks of her cheekbones and down the plush sides of her cheeks. Tracing the edges of her face with his long fingers. Just looking at her.

"What?" she whispered.

"I want to remember you like this," he replied. His eyes darkened with emotion and his voice deepened. "I know this is your choice, and I'm so excited to see you as a goblin. I think you suit more to that life than anything else. But... Well. This is how I want to remember you, too. As the woman I met who was so brave that she was willing to walk into the goblin court without fear."

Her heart warmed nearly to pain. "I'll still be the same person, Lux."

"I know you will." He leaned forward and pressed his lips to her forehead, and then he was gone.

He darted away from her, making sure he was low on the ground and tucked behind the brush. None of the guards would see him without the sunlight to guide their gaze. Their torches didn't penetrate through the shadows of the forest beyond.

The temple sat in a clearing just ahead. Though the building was more wooden in structure than she would have expected. Temples were marble in the mortal realm, but here? Apparently they were built out of the remains of giant trees. The roof arched upwards on the sides, like the building itself was wearing a giant hat. And a tree had wrapped itself around the back of the building, growing into the temple as though they were one. Warm wood made up the walls and was covered in fairy lights. The temple glowed at nighttime, and that made it all the more difficult for Esther to sneak into it without being seen.

It was better than daylight, she supposed. At least she could get a little closer without fearing they would see her coming.

She heard the first rock whistle through the air. A bush not too far from the guards rattled and one split from the others to investigate. This goblin man had tusks erupting from his bottom lip, and he was certainly larger than most goblins she'd seen. He wore leather armor and held a spear in his hand with a wicked tip.

"What is it?" Another guard called out. This one had fur over his entire body, striped black and orange like a jungle cat.

"Not sure," the tusked guard replied with a grunt. "I can't see anything."

The tiger-bodied man sighed and wandered over to the other guard. "Here, let me hold a light for you. It's probably just a rabbit."

Lux let fly another stone, and the next bush rattled much louder than the first. He must be throwing large rocks to make that much noise.

The last guard saw the way the bush violently moved, and that must have been enough for him to get involved. He snorted—was that a pig nose?—and then wandered over to join his friends with concern for who was luring them away from the temple. They obviously didn't consider that someone else might be right behind them, but that worked in her advantage.

Esther rushed across the wooden stairs, hopped over

the fence, and then ducked into the darkened opening that led into the rest of the temple. Sure, if anyone had been watching they would have known she was no assassin. The grace that was required to do all the things she'd done was severely lacking, but she got inside the temple without the guards noticing her, hadn't she?

A large blanket covered the doorway, in what she assumed was a fancier door than she was used to. No problem at all, because she could slip beneath the bottom right corner and no one would be the wiser. By the time they turned around, the fabric would have stopped moving. Her plan was foolproof.

Esther was quite proud of herself for thinking on her toes. Freya would have been as well, if her sister was here.

If only her sister was here.

A pang of homesickness stabbed her in the chest. Freya would have hated every second of this dangerous quest. She'd be arguing the whole way, but then she would have buckled down and gotten everything done in record time. Her sister was impressive like that.

Esther supposed she had gotten some of those skills from Freya as well. Look at her now! She'd snuck into this temple without a single guard knowing.

She backed away from the swaying fabric and turned around to feast her eyes on the interior of the temple. The building was filled with still pools of water. They looked like glass panels on the floor until a slow glide of a fish fin rose through them. Not even the animals within those pools created ripples, as if the magic wouldn't allow such an embarrassment.

Torches lit the space with red and orange light that

bounced off the exaggerated golden columns, guiding the eye all the way to the end of the single room. There was an altar there with something that looked like a coffin. She could see the bright white light emanating from the depths of whatever that coffin contained. And behind it all was a giant mural depicting a battle scene of thousands. Fae fought against fae, with powerful bolts of light shooting from their hands.

She'd have to ask Lux what battle was depicted here, but she had a feeling she could guess. Someone had tried to take all the magic for themselves, but that wasn't how magic worked. And it didn't want to be used like that.

No matter, she didn't have time to wonder about the history of the Autumn Court. She needed to get to that altar so she could beg it to turn her into a goblin. Then all would be well.

Except, there was no path to the altar. Nothing but pools of water with thin golden frames to separate the pools from each other. Not a single one of those thin lines would hold her weight, which meant she had to walk through the water to get there.

It felt wrong to step her toe into the depths. Esther didn't have another choice. She hiked her shirts up and gently stepped into the water.

Not a single ripple spread from her touch either. She winced at the cool touch that glided up her legs all the way to her waist. Without ripples, it looked very much like she was becoming part of the water. She couldn't tell where she started and where the water ended. Torchlight glimmered on the surface and spread all the way up her body.

Was she magic now? Were these waters the thing that gave all the goblins their impossible power? And if so, would it devour her whole for daring to bathe within its depths?

She reached the first mesh barrier. Small steps led up to it, so it was easy for her to step over it and descend into the next pool.

Esther hissed out a long breath as her toes touched the next square of water. This one wasn't cold. It was boiling hot. She moved as quickly as possible through this one, but her skin was still bright red and burning as she clambered up the second set of stairs. Only one more pool to get through before she could walk up onto that altar. She feared this one might take the skin from her bones.

The frigid, icy water was welcome after the burning. Though, by the time she reached the altar, she was ready to be out of the cold again. Lukewarm, boiling, then frozen. The magic was trying to tell her something, she thought. Or maybe she was just making all this up in her head and the waters were a deterrent for those who thought to steal from this well.

A torch to her right popped. A shower of sparks fell in front of her, and Esther tossed her arm up to avoid the burning embers. When she lowered it, the coffin had disappeared. The altar steps led to something she'd expected.

A wishing well. Just like she'd thought she would find.

The burning white light had dimmed into a blueish purple glow that was welcoming. Comforting. Almost like the magic wanted her to be there, or at least didn't mind that she'd come to it.

She ascended the last step toward her new destiny.

CHAPTER 13

The magic in the well called out to her. It was strange, though. Esther wasn't sure she could actually hear a voice whispering. It was almost like her mind had given the magic a voice because she couldn't understand it in any other way.

But there was no sound.

Only a sensation in her head that someone else was taking up space within her mind and guiding her thoughts in the direction it wanted her to think. She might have been uncomfortable having someone else inside her head, but it wasn't an ominous kind of presence.

The magic was soft around the edges. That's the only way she could think to describe it. The being inside her head didn't want to hurt her. It didn't want to scare her, either. It simply wanted to dip into her mind and understand why she had come all this way just to see a magical pool.

Perhaps it didn't get many visitors, though she

suspected that wasn't true at all. If she had known of a magical wishing well in her realm, then Esther was certain thousands of people would have flocked to it every year just to beg for help.

Maybe mortals needed more help from magical deities than the fae.

She set her hands on the sides of the well, peering down into the depths of glittering water far beyond her reach. With a soft sigh, she let her wish fly from her lips and bounce down the stones all the way to the pool.

"I wish to become a goblin."

The words sounded strange to her when they echoed back. Or maybe that was the presence in her mind showing her its own confusion.

Who wanted to become a goblin? She was a beautiful young woman with her whole life ahead of her. With a face like hers, she could marry a nobleman and live in comfort until she died.

Flashes of another future played before her eyes. A life with a handsome young man who liked to ride horses around his expansive estate. The grass was always green where he lived, and the sky was always blue. A white chateau loomed in the distance, impossibly pretty and well maintained by a staff nearing one hundred people. Her husband was a good man, though he might be a little boring at times. She didn't like to talk to him about anything other than horses, because that was his only passion. Everything else was lesser.

Esther might have children with him. Tiny, bouncing blonde girls who tumbled over the emerald green grass when their father wasn't looking.

But even as she watched this lavish future flash in front of her, Esther knew that wasn't what she wanted. Every time she saw the image of herself, she saw how sad she was. How unhappy. Living like that would drain the soul from her body until she was nothing but a husk of a woman. Nothing at all like herself.

And Esther quite liked the wild, mad creature she was becoming. She enjoyed being free and without chains. This tamed version of herself wasn't who she wanted to see in the future.

"No," she replied, as if she were having a conversation with the wishing well. "That's not what I want. I don't want to be that person you're showing me, either. That's the person my mother wanted me to be. It wasn't my wish."

She could almost hear the "Ah" that echoed through her mind. The wishing well understood that sometimes a mother wanted what was best for her child, but in reality, that best would only squash the greatest desires of her child.

Esther wasn't meant to be the little wife that everyone thought was so pretty, but also so maintained.

The thoughts in her head jumbled, shifting so quickly that she had to clutch the sides of the wishing well so she didn't tumble over the edge and plunge into the waters below. Though the well had allowed her to go through the other waters, she didn't think it would enjoy her being within it.

Finally her thoughts slowed again, and this time an image was thrust in front of her with a triumphant echo.

She blinked through a sudden headache, trying to understand what the well wanted her to see this time.

It was her and her sister.

Freya walked into the living room of their home with a bright smile on her face. "Esther!" she called out. "Did you see this yet? The gardens are growing with so many butterflies this year. I thought we could walk through them and count how many were born today. We're going to have a veritable army if they keep going like this."

Her heart swelled two times its size. Freya loved being outside, and she loved making sure that their home was something that still inspired Esther. Even though they didn't always see issues the same, they always made up in the end.

Maybe that's what she'd forgotten when she ran away here. Though Freya and her were very different people, they still loved each other so much. And that love had gotten Esther through a lot more trying times than any other love in her life.

If she turned into a goblin, she would never see this life again. She might never see her sister again, because Freya hated goblins. Freya hated everything that had to do with magic.

She'd never be a sister again. Not, at least, to the woman who was her blood.

"Freya never wanted this," she whispered into the well. "But Freya likes a boring life. She enjoys getting up every day and seeing the same thing over and over again. It was driving me mad and every time I told her that, she brushed me aside like I was too young to understand what life really is."

The magic insistently shoved in her head until she could almost hear words.

A strange, warbled voice said, "Freya never wanted boredom either, but she wanted to make sure that you were safe."

That wasn't at all the truth. Her sister liked being no one. Freya didn't want anyone to know she or her sister existed, and she would have kept it that way until the two of them were rotting somewhere underneath that cabin. No one could change Freya's mind, no matter how hard they tried.

Esther gripped the edge of the well harder until she felt the stone bite into her palms. "It's not what I want."

Another deep hum echoed through the stones. It bounced all around her until she didn't know where the sound had echoed from. Behind her? Was someone standing behind her this entire time?

But then another new vision flashed and Esther couldn't turn around to see if someone was breathing down her neck. This vision was far too captivating, and it made her entire heart and body sing.

She saw herself in the forest of the Autumn Court. Lux clambered down from the treehouse, although he looked older than he did now. Fine wrinkles had spread out around his eyes and mouth from many years of laughter and happiness.

He crouched down into the crinkling leaves and held his arms wide. A tiny creature ran toward him with all the speed of a cheetah. This goblin boy had a tail like a monkey and ears that were bigger than dinner plates. He crawled into Lux's arm and held his arms around his father's neck as Lux stood.

Sure, they were a strange sight. Lux with his rat-like features and the little monkey boy in his arms. But it made her entire body soften with so much love.

This was the future she wanted. Lux and an odd child grinning at her. It was the only life she wanted, really, when there were so many other options for her at this crossroads.

The vision turned around a bit, and she saw herself. A plume of white bushed out behind her. As the vision strode by, Esther got to see that she'd grown a tail. A big, white fluffy tail.

Sure, the sight of that made Esther a little uncomfortable. She didn't know anyone that would see such a large physical difference and be able to brush it off without a flinch. Could she even get used to having a tail? How did one walk around with that attached to their body?

But also, it looked quite nice. The white fur was obviously soft. She thought the entire package on her body looked rather regal. Like the faeries of old that would appear out of the forest and offer people a spell that would make their lives better. Rather than a troll person who would drag children underneath her bridge and turn them into monsters.

"Yes," she said into the magical waters. "That's the life I want."

It seemed a little confused that she had so readily agreed.

The presence twisted around in her head, trying to convey some message that appeared in the form of her own lips muttering, "You cannot turn back from a change like this. Once goblin, there is no mortal."

She was fine with that. Esther took only one more moment to think about her past life and the person she was now. She stretched her arms over her head, enjoying the feeling of being human for a few more seconds before she leaned over the edge of the well and grinned down at the sparkling waters.

"I don't want to stay a mortal and being a goblin would be the greatest gift anyone has ever given me. Turn me into a monster, magic. If that's what you think I will be." Esther shrugged. "Monster or not, I'll finally be happy."

And there it was. All laid out with a bow on top because that's how she felt. As a mortal, as a human, she couldn't be happy. Esther needed the adventure that came with being a goblin. The freedom that no one would take her back, because they couldn't, and she shouldn't feel bad about that.

Becoming a goblin meant she got to own her own life without feeling guilty. She could become something more, something other, and no human would ever force her to return to the life where she didn't feel like herself.

The presence warmed. She heard a long sigh in her head, felt a pulse of happiness that mimicked her own, and then the presence left her mind. It was just Esther standing beside a wishing well once again. And hoping that the presence understood she wasn't doing this because of some romantic ideal. She wasn't doing this because she wanted Lux to love her more.

Esther's choice was entirely selfish. The benefits that came with it were just a side effect of her own choice.

The sparkling light rose from the well. Tiny bubbles surrounded her, each one glistening with iridescent colors that she thought might be the magic itself. One floated close to her nose and gently bumped the tip. It popped, and all she saw were a thousand stars falling from the sky. The sparkling light settled on her shoulders, in her hair, and a fine layer of magic turned her skin to starlight and glistening sparkles.

The transformation from mortal to goblin woman was painless and easy. She'd thought it might hurt, but instead, it just felt like someone had removed a great weight from her shoulders.

Esther wasn't herself anymore. She was a woman with a tail and a heart full of hope. Finally, after all this time, Esther could be herself.

Reaching behind her back, Esther stroked a hand over the luxurious tail that had grown from the base of her spine. She'd been right about guessing the texture in the vision. It did feel like rabbit fur, soft and velvety to the touch.

Strangely, it didn't feel odd to have a tail attached to her body. It was like her mind knew what to do with it no matter that it was new. She wagged it behind herself, then giggled at the odd sensation.

"Thank you," she whispered.

"You're whole now." The voice erupted from the well, though the words were softer at the end. As though something was moving farther away from her.

"Wait!" Esther called out. "Why did you give me a tail like this?"

The response was grumbled, as though the well was unused to speaking out loud. "Because above all else, Esther, you are loyal and kind. A good companion to all who meet you. This was the only animal to mix your spirit with. A kind, loyal, and giving creature who watches over all that are given to it."

Yes, that sounded right. She was whole and her entire being filled with that knowledge until she was fairly bursting with happiness. Whole. Finally, the right way on the outside when she had been struggling with herself all her life.

She couldn't wait to show Lux.

CHAPTER 14

*A*ll the pools of water had evened out in temperature. If Esther couldn't see the water herself, she would have assumed she was walking through air. She waded through the water and stepped out on the other side, then gasped as her clothing dried instantly.

Even the fur of her tail puffed back up to normal size. As if she'd never touched the water at all.

"Magic," she whispered. "How fascinating."

Now, she and Lux hadn't talked about how she was going to get out of the temple. The guards must have returned to their posts by now, and she had no way to let Lux know that she was finished within the walls of this enchanted place.

Shoot. Here she had been, gloating, certain that they'd planned out a foolproof way of her becoming a goblin, only to realize that she had been so very wrong. Freya would have laughed at her sister for thinking that this plan was without fault. Goodness, Freya would have seen this being a problem from a mile away.

And Esther didn't know why she was thinking of Freya so much lately. She'd left her sister behind and knew better than to entertain that pain in her chest. Freya would not come to the faerie realm. Yes, Esther could miss her. But that wouldn't change what she'd done and no matter what, Freya was lost to her now.

She'd made her choice. Now she had to live with it.

Sighing, she lifted the very edge of the fabric door and peeked out into the shadows. The three guards were back at their post. She could just see around their backs where they stood at attention. Although, they looked bored.

Damn. How was she supposed to let Lux know she was done?

Magic wasn't exactly at her fingertips yet. She had no idea how to cast spells or use whatever magic being a goblin woman gave her. If she did, then maybe she could have sent a message to Lux and let him know.

The bushes rattled to the right again, but this time, it wasn't a rock.

Lux popped out of the shadows with a wild expression on his face. Obviously he'd seen her peek out from behind the guards and was doing what she had told him not to do. He was putting himself at risk so she could get away.

That damned man was going to make her heart pop out of her chest, with love and with worry that he'd do something stupid.

Like this.

He waved his arms over his head. "Hey! Were you looking for me earlier?"

The guards looked at each other and then back at the daring goblin boy who tried to get their attention.

The guard with the tusks cleared his throat, then leaned to the side and muttered, "Is he insane?"

"I think that's Lux," the furred guard replied. "You know, Horace's boy? The one that he was always going on about and how he couldn't follow the rules."

The previous guard sighed, then nodded. "All right. Let's teach him a lesson then."

A part of Esther couldn't believe they would hurt Lux. They knew his father, for heaven's sake. Obviously these guards would have no ill intent, and she could trail along behind them in the woods until they finished with Lux. Then, she would get him and they would return to his treehouse, ready to live their lives as they had planned.

But the guards descended on him with madness in their eyes. They grabbed her goblin boy and shook him so hard she heard his neck crack with the movement.

"What are you doing here, boy?" The tiger-skinned goblin snarled. "You know what your father would tell us to do? He'd say lock him up for the night. Let real rats feast on his flesh, and in the morning when there's naught but pieces left of him, pull him out and put him back together with magic. Then do it all again to make sure the lesson stuck."

Her stomach heaved. They were going to let rats chew on him? They didn't mind putting a man through that much pain because he'd played a prank on them?

Lux met her eyes, staring at her with a wild grin on

his own face. "Do your worst, boys. I'm waiting for the most perfect girl any of us have ever met, and if that means you have to take me to your terrifying prison, then memories of her will keep me warm at night."

The tusked guard snorted. "He's lost his damn mind, poor boy. I say we toss him in, anyway. No rest for the wicked and all that."

Esther didn't think he used that term correctly, and she wasn't about to let them toss Lux into a prison. He was too important to her, and frankly, she was ready to save his butt for the first time.

Flipping the curtain back from the doorway, she dramatically stepped out into the torchlight beyond the temple. Taking a deep breath, she crossed her arms over her chest like she'd seen Freya and her mother do so many times and cleared her throat.

"Gentleman," she scolded. "Exactly what are you doing with Lux?"

All three of the guards froze, then turned as one to stare at her. Lux was already mouthing for her to run, but she wasn't going to do that this time.

Esther was the hero at this moment. She was going to defeat these villains as they'd never been defeated before. Which was to say that she would convince them, calmly and like an adult, that they needed to release Lux so that she could take him back home where they would live out their lives in the most romantic way possible.

And if they didn't let him go, then she would threaten to ruin the wishing well.

Which she wouldn't ever do, of course. But they didn't know that.

"Who are you?" the tusked guard snarled.

"My name is Esther. I'm with Lux."

The guards looked at each other again, whispered a few things, and then the tusked guard replied. "Are you the little mortal girl that was foolish enough to make a deal with a goblin?"

"I'm not foolish," she replied, already bristling at their tone.

The tiger-skinned guard snorted. "Yeah, that's her, then. Lux! We thought you were playing a prank on us, but you let a mortal into the temple? You know that's the worst kind of transgression and comes with the worst kind of punishment. Now you're going to deal with someone a lot worse than us."

Esther's mind worked tenfold. She couldn't let them put him in prison, or worse. But she also refused to let them touch him anymore at all.

She needed her wits about her. She needed to be more like her sister, who always thought quickly on her feet. How many times had Freya talked Esther out of a bad situation with the townsfolk?

What would Freya do?

Esther cleared her throat, reached behind herself, and wrapped her tail around her waist. "Guards, do I look like a mortal woman?"

They eyed her tail, then looked back at each other with confused expressions. "Mortals don't have tails, do they?" the tiger guard asked.

"I don't think so," the tusked one replied.

The third still had said nothing, but she wasn't all that sure he knew how to speak. His pig snout might not allow him to make noises like that, and he was eyeing her with the most amount of distrust.

She could do this.

She could trick them into thinking that she'd always been like this, and that they had to let Lux go. All she needed was to talk them into a circle and then they could run.

"You said that mortals weren't allowed in the temple, but obviously I am not a mortal." She flicked her tail to emphasize the words. "And if you think Lux was trying to pull a prank on you, how do you know that? He wasn't here until the moment he leapt out of those bushes. I saw that for myself. You have no proof of any other deeds committed by my husband."

The tusked guard lifted a finger, releasing his hold on Lux. "Well now, that's not entirely correct. Those same bushes were shifting earlier and made all of us leave our posts."

"And yet, you didn't see Lux at that time. Did you?" She raised a brow. "Out with it. Did you see Lux?"

"No," he grumbled.

The tiger guard released Lux as well and took a heavy step toward her. "He might have been distracting us so you could sneak into the temple."

Damn, they were smarter than they looked. Perhaps they had chosen the best of the best to guard this temple after all.

Esther swallowed hard. "Do you have any proof of that either? If you didn't see me enter the temple, then you have no idea if I was mortal when I entered, or goblin. Which can only mean that I didn't break any rules at all. Because you didn't see me break rules."

"Is that the way things go?" He looked at the tiger guard, who shrugged.

"A rule cannot be broken if no one sees it break." Esther nodded firmly. As if she had any idea what she was talking about.

The pig-faced guard snorted and released Lux as well. "I'd like it known that what you just said isn't the way things go, miss. A rule is always broken if someone breaks it. You know if you broke the rule, and you saw yourself do it, so you better come out with it right now and tell us what you did so we can punish the both of you appropriately."

Except, they had all let Lux go. Her goblin boy backed away from all of them, then nodded his head toward the woods. She knew exactly what he wanted her to do, and she knew it was the right step to take.

"I don't think you're right," she replied with a grin. "I think rules are meant to be broken though, so we won't see eye to eye on this."

Esther burst into movement. She launched over the stairs and back into the brush she'd first snuck out of. Her tail flipped behind her, and likely the sound of her laughter trailed through the wind. She couldn't stop herself from laughing, though. This was the very first time she'd been able to feel free and wild.

She loved it.

Esther ran through the woods for so many lungfuls of wild air that she didn't know how long it took her to flee from the guards. Then someone leaned around a tree and wrapped his firm arm around her waist.

She didn't scream. Why would she need to? She knew that iron band of muscle as though it were her own soul grabbing her out of the darkness.

With a solid thud, she landed hard on Lux's chest and curled into the safe hold of his body. He wrapped his arms around her waist tightly and drew her into the shadow of the tree trunk. Together, they waited until they couldn't hear the guard's frantic footsteps any longer.

"You brave, foolish woman," Lux muttered against her neck where he pressed his lips. "You saved me."

"Well, I thought eventually I should repay you for all the times you've saved me." She leaned away from him, forcing his lips to release themselves from the lingering warmth on the base of her throat. "Besides, I couldn't bear the thought of rats chewing on your flesh."

"They wouldn't. They know one of their own." He tunneled his fingers through her hair, gently scooping into her blonde curls. "You're a goblin now," he whispered in awe.

"I am." She flicked her tail at his arm around her waist. "What do you think?"

"I think you're lovelier than moonlight and more beautiful than all the stars in the sky." He kissed her forehead, her cheeks, then gently laid a single kiss to her lips. "My goblin bride."

CHAPTER 15

*T*hey'd fallen into a very comfortable routine together in their treehouse home. Esther hadn't thought it would be so easy, but somehow the sight of the two of them together had made many goblins in Lux's village believe he'd finally grown up.

In every aspect, they were the cutest couple here. No one could convince her otherwise.

And though she still missed her home sometimes, Lux had made it very easy for her to forget the things she'd liked in the mortal realm, and focus entirely on the things she loved here.

Like him.

She still woke up every morning and had no idea how she'd gotten this lucky. Lux made her happy on a level she hadn't realized was possible. Her heart wouldn't let her make any other choice but him, after all. Esther had learned to trust her heart.

Lux poked his head above the ladder to their home and gave her a bright grin. "Are you ready, or what?"

"I'm just about ready. Someone told me we were going on a picnic much later than he should have, or we would already have something to eat on said picnic." She rolled her eyes for dramatic effect, but knew he wouldn't take it that she was angry.

He liked to surprise her with little afternoon adventures at every chance he could. Sometimes they wandered through the Autumn Court in search of more dangerous faeries to spy on. Sometimes, like today, he just wanted to spend time with her.

She already knew he'd have a thousand questions to ask her. What did she do today? Was she still happy here? What new goblin had she fallen madly in love with?

The answer to the last question was always the same. She never fell in love with any goblin. Not at all. But today was the perfect day to admit that she had fallen in love with him. Madly, deeply, and without question.

"Well, hurry up! We're going to lose all the light and I want to make sure you get to enjoy the sun since you've been avoiding it forever." He clambered back down the ladder with laughter trailing behind him.

She wasn't avoiding the sun. Esther picked up the pack of food and swung it over her shoulder. The man would be the death of her, she swore. She was helping out one of the goblins because they needed someone to grind herbs that would go in a few poultices. That was the only reason she hadn't seen the sun in a few days.

But Lux knew how much she loved it, and he wanted her to see it every single day.

She followed him out of the treehouse and then sprinted after him when he took off through the undergrowth. Now that she was a goblin, Esther could run a lot longer than before. Her legs never seemed to get tired, her lungs never heaved for breath. She was stronger in every sense of the term.

This path differed from their normal journey. Lux had never taken her all the way from the Autumn Court like this, and when they burst out into an emerald green meadow, she was shocked to see it dotted with tiny white flowers. In the distance, a dark castle loomed with sharp spires and a galaxy of stars behind it.

"Where are we?" she asked, breathless with awe.

"This is the Goblin Kingdom." Lux opened his arms wide and gestured all around them. "The Goblin King lives here, with a very limited staff. He doesn't want too many people living outside of their courts, says it's something to do with happiness. But anyway. I knew you hadn't seen it yet, and I think it's the perfect place to have a comfortable picnic."

"Wow." She looked at the sky as it changed colors from a bright, vivid purple to a deep blue. "I've never seen a sky do that before."

"No one else has. The Goblin King designed this entire kingdom to be exactly as he wants it." Lux reached for her pack and pulled out a blanket.

With a flourish, Lux flipped the blanket out and then helped her set all their food out on the red and white checkered blanket. It was perfect, this moment between her and him. Like they were a real family.

She flopped down beside him when he finished and put her head in his lap. "Lux, can you ask me the question you always ask?"

"How are you liking being in the goblin realm?" He ran his fingers through her hair.

"No, the other one."

A twinkled appeared in his eyes, like he already knew what she was going to say. "What did you do today?"

Esther laughed. "No! Silly."

"Oh, oh." The expression on his face turned very serious, and his eyes watched her carefully so she knew he didn't want to miss a single moment of her next words. "Did you fall in love with any goblins today?"

"I did." She reached up and cupped the back of his neck, drawing him down closer to her. "I fell in love with you."

"Good," he whispered, just a hair's breadth from her lips. "Because you are the sun in my daylight and the stars in my midnight. I love you, Esther. And I cannot wait to spend the rest of our lives together."

He kissed her like a starving man, and she devoured every kiss he would feed her. Esther had no idea how long they lay together in the sun, but she knew that she was painfully happy.

She loved him. He loved her. Their story was only just beginning.

Until a shout ran through the meadow. "Esther!"

She thought she knew that voice. Esther released her hold on the goblin boy and sat up, hair wild around her face.

With a breathless gasp, she pressed her hand against her lips. "Freya?"

Freya's story begins in Of Goblins and Gold, where you'll

follow Freya and a Goblin King on an adventure that will surely set your heart aflame.

Don't miss the next STOLEN BRIDES OF THE FAE book!

THE STORY CONTINUES...

Continue Freya's story in...

Of Goblins and Gold

ABOUT THE AUTHOR

Emma Hamm is a small town girl on a blueberry field in Maine. She writes stories that remind her of home, of fairytales, and of myths and legends that make her mind wander.

She can be found by the fireplace with a cup of tea and her two Maine Coon cats dipping their paws into the water without her knowing.

Subscribe to my Newsletter for updates on new stories!
www.emmahamm.com

facebook.com/EmmaHammAuthor
twitter.com/EmmaHammAuthor
instagram.com/emmahammauthor

Printed in Great Britain
by Amazon

61471615R00081